TALES FROM THE EDGE OF MAYBE

Published by Kooky Cat Books 2025
Copyright 2023 Martii [M.A.] Maclean
Kooky Cat books

A catalogue record for this book is available from the National Library of Australia.

Formatting and cover design by Kooky Cat Books

Second edition 2025
ISBN 978-0-9876442-8-2

TALES FROM THE EDGE OF MAYBE

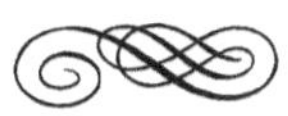

M A MACLEAN

For Trevor and Minerva,
always ready for adventure
on our travels through space and time.

Contents

1

One Thousand Years

Mayla swam upwards through an acrid fizz of static. A tiny part of her brain observed the two concepts — swimming and static—don't fit together. Dreams don't need to make sense, she assured herself, though they can feel very real.

'Good morning,' said a wet, mechanical voice, out of sight at the edge of Mayla's fading dream. 'Welcome to ... being awake.'

'Good morning,' she murmured, feeling like dust was blowing off her vocal cords.

'Good morning,' clicked a second dream voice, more mechanical. 'We estimate you have slept approximately one thousand years.'

Mayla ignored the dream voices, swallowed, her throat dry like a pavement on a summer day. She wanted to plunge back into her dream and swim. She tried rolling to doze again, but couldn't move. As she strained, the static from the dream grew tangible, became a burning. She tried to move again but her body felt like stone. Each effort turned her nerves to flame. Heart thumping—frantic. Lungs squeezed, crackled, and sour air wafted up her throat and crept into the back of her nose. The static and the acridness of her dream were real and part of her.

'Sleeper 957, you are functioning within optimal parameters ... allowing for variations due to harvest events—'

'Hush, Remi.' Wet voice. The mechanical voice clicked to an abrupt stop. Mayla tried to turn in the direction of these voices—no—tried to open her eyes—no. Her parched breath puffed out in panicked chunks. A keening whine rose in her dry throat.

'Mayla...you are safe...I am Devin...you are safe. Be patient, concentrate on calming your breath. Try moving your fingers for me and wiggle your toes. Your body will be in your control again soon enough.'

Sending messages from her panicked brain, trying to count and slow her breathing, willing her fingers to move, pleading with her eyes to open. Her face felt like stone, no, it felt like nothing. Her skin, her flesh, felt absent. She visualised the muscles of her forehead tugging upward to draw her eyes open. All she managed was to make her eyelids spark and burn, at least it was a sensation. Then something more—tears tracking down, trickling into her ear. They tickled and she made a strangled laughing sound with the relief of this scintilla of sensation. Now there was a burning in her hands and feet. It was spreading, leaking up her legs, up her arms. What would happen to her if the burning wasn't stopped.

'Good,' said the Devin voice. 'You are moving your fingers.'

'Estimated time to full return of function, seventy-four minutes thirty-seven seconds,' the mechanical Remi voice.

'W-w-h-at?' she rasped.

'Inquiry,' said Remi.

Devin made another wetly mechanical approximation of shushing his companion and Mayla's heart sped up again. *Where am I? What's going on?*

'You'd like to know what happened, of course.' The Devin voice was kind but starched, stiffened. 'You have been suffering from a ... condition, but you are recovering now.'

'The plague vector was unknown,' Remi chanted. 'Afflicting approximately twenty-seven percent of global population.'

Mayla tried to query plague, but only managed a gagging whimper.

'Plague is an inappropriate term,' Devin corrected. 'The condition began globally and spread as a virus would. It was first considered a death event.'

'Total cessation of life indicators,' Remi interjected.

'Yes,' gentled Devin. 'Those stricken ceased living ... simply and inexplicably, ceased all biological function. No cause or cure could be found. The word plague became the accepted vernacular.'

Who the hell are these people? She tried again to move her hands, grunted with effort, her arms burned then there was a cool dry touch. She shivered, tried to move away.

'You felt my hand,' said Devin. 'Well done, Mayla. Now your toes.' Another touch. She recoiled. They could touch her anywhere, in any way they chose and she was powerless to stop them. 'You will be fully awake soon, but I need you to compose yourself ... this situation will be a challenge ... but remember, you are safe.'

Gritting her teeth, she breathed, calmed, waited. Now light glowed through her frozen eyelids. She flexed her toes, her feet buzzed and ribbons of heat snaked up her calves. Her fingers tingled as she wiggled them. Sensation crept up each arm and across her shoulders. One eyelid twitched, then the other. Straining her brows upward, her jammed eyes opened, slowly, trembling. Her vision swirling. Shapes and shadows became doors and cabinets. A too bright circle of light from above made her eyes ache.

'Your eyes are open, well done,' said the Devin voice. 'I will reduce the illumination.'

In the gloom outside the circle of light, there was movement. It must be this Devin. She pushed hard, but her head still wouldn't turn. 'Who are you?' she rasped. 'Where am I?'

The shadowy figure moved closer to her. 'I'm Devin.'

'I am Remi,' said the other voice from the shadows. 'We are your caretakers.'

'I'm your ... nurse,' corrected Devin. 'And this place is a Burrow Unit.'

'Burrow?' Mayla tongue felt like mud. 'Plague?'

'We will answer all your questions. I know you are frightened ... it is of great importance to us that you understand you are safe.'

'Much has changed while you were in time stasis,' said Remi.

'I don't—' A fiery swirl of hurt blossomed in her gut. Mayla groaned trying to tuck herself into a ball to squeeze away the throbbing pain.

'You have pain. One moment,' said Devin. There was a cold tingle at Mayla's throat and the pain began to fade. 'Pain is unpleasant, but it tells me your awakening is progressing well.'

'Metabolism is recommencing,' said Remi. 'Tissue regeneration is evident.'

'Tissue?' Mayla sobbed. Everything hurt, she couldn't move. She didn't know these strange people. *Where was Michael? Why were these nurses saying such bizarre things?*

There was a trickle of warmth on her lips, her tongue. She swallowed. 'Some herbal ... tea, to calm you,' said Devin.

His gloom-lit face smiled down at her. 'The tea will only flow slowly from the tube. Take small swallows while I tell you the story of your sleeping.'

She sipped, swallowed.

'There was an extraordinary event,' said Devin. 'In one day, it impacted almost one quarter of the people of Earth. The world watched in horror as so many fell victim. There was nothing for families ... for loved ones to do but mourn and lay the dead to rest. But with so many victims needing ceremonies, they needed to wait, and in the waiting, it became evident that these seemingly dead bodies did not degenerate. They remained ... present... whole... unchanged.'

'No decomposition of corporeal form. Not alive. Not dead.'

'Hush, Remi.' Devin continued. 'The not-dead had no place, so the families took their sleeping loved ones' home and put them ... to bed.'

'For the sleepers without family it was a different fate,' said Remi.

'Remi, enough. De-briefing as the sleeper awakens is my responsibility. Please, attend to your duties.'

'I will communicate the progress of 957 to Zone Control.'

'You will tell Zone Control that *Mayla* has awakened.' There was clicking near Devin, from Devin, she wasn't sure.

More clicking somewhere in the gloom, and Remi said, 'I will tell Zone Control about Mayla.'

'Control?' rasped Mayla. 'Where—'

'Sip and listen, Mayla,' said Devin, smiling down at her. 'I will tell of your sleeping days as best I can.'

Fresh panic rose, she sobbed, choking on the trickling tea. Devin moved again and there was another cold tingle at her throat and she felt calm, detached, curious.

'You are safe,' said Devin and his story continued. 'At first, chaos. One quarter of all the peoples of Earth, regardless of age, gender or locality, fell victim to this unfathomable condition. People feared contagion. In places were superstition was stronger than science, many sleepers were burned in hopes of being rid of any possible biological danger. With time, and the discovery of a lack of biological degradation in the victims, fear turned to curiosity, then sleepers were confiscated and studied by the authorities.'

'What caused it?'

'Initial observations showed very little. The only commonality was that the sleepers were all found outside. The studies show each sleeper had a fungus present in their lungs and throughout the body.'

'One thousand years of extrapolation, leads to the strongest theory,' added Remi.

'Thank you, Remi.' More clicking and Devin continued the explanation. 'There was much research. Cosmological records of the period show unusual waves of plasma and what has been termed a Quantum Ripple, a fluctuation of the Earth's magnetic field. The field destabilised for twenty-one hours. During this time the Earth was less protected. The plasma wave penetrated the atmosphere. We are as certain as we can be that the Quantum Ripple transformed the fungus which caused the cessation of this random group of humans in preparation for the rebalancing.'

'Rebalancing?' Every answer spawned swarms of questions. Frustration spiked through the induced calm. Mayla squeezed her fists.

'Clenched fists.' Remi buzzed. 'Progress.'

'Hush, Remi. Observations should be made and noted in a less intrusive manner,' said Devin. 'Answering Mayla's questions takes precedence.'

'The rebalancing is part of the story you have slept through. I will try to explain. I'm sure you were aware of the ways in which the Earth was being exploited, damaged and overburdened in your time.'

'Yes.'

'Earth is an energetic and organic system. The magnetic fields and the atmosphere protect all life here. This planet works to stay in balance and protect the organisms that live on it. Through ignorance and disregard, humans had done much damage. The Earth needed to maintain that balance. Some rebalancing events may seem brutal, dangerous weather, deadly diseases, but they allowed the earth-system to survive.'

'But I ...' Mayla struggled to form a question.

'The sleeping virus was the first event. Others followed over the centuries, viral, environmental, social. Each event drastically reduced the human population.'

'They're gone?' Mayla sobbed.

'You are not alone.' Devin's cool hand was on her shoulder. 'Many of the sleepers are now waking.'

'We have taken readings as they regained metabolic function,' blurted Remi. 'Energy fluctuations surround each sleeper, resonating deeply into tissue of the body, the nervous system and brain.'

Devin clicked. Remi stopped. 'We theorise the sleepers were held in stasis by the planet, so that they would endure the chaos and wake to live on in the rebalanced world.'

'My family?'

'Your family took you home, they kept you safe. As you remained ... sleeping and your loved ones grew older, you were held in trust by your family group.'

'Archives show you were passed through three generations,' added Remi.

'Things had become complicated by then. Many families, like yours, struggled with the climate, hunger, others hardships. Many communities banded together and placed sleepers in shelters. Funding for these became scarce as hardships increased.'

'After your community failed, records show you were salvaged,' chirped Remi.

'Salvaged?' *What the hell?*

'When communities were unable to shelter their sleepers, churches saved them. Believing their mission was divine, they justified the exploitation as a means to finance the good works. They used the sleepers as part of their greater good. This took funds. They needed to use the resources the sleepers had to offer and declared benevolent guardianship over their charges.'

'What does all that mean?' Mayla choked out the words and struggled to breathe.

'The trustees took donations.' Devin paused, quiet whirring. 'Parts from sleepers were sold to help pay for the protection they offered.'

'Eyes, liver tissue, kidney, ovum,' mumbled Remi.

'Parts?' Mayla's heart cavorted. A monitor buzzed.

'Remi.' Click-click. 'Mayla's story needs to offer relief to her curiosity, and resolution as she regains and re-enters her life.'

Mayla groaned, straining to move her arms, to feel and discover if she was whole. 'What did they take? What did they do?'

'We have restored you to a full and complete state,' said Remi.

'What?' Mayla struggled to rise from her bed. Toppled sideways, and was caught by cold, soft hands and helped back on to the bed.

Another sting at her throat. 'Sip, Mayla,' cooed Devin. 'I will tell you.' There was a quiet whirring. 'An eye — which we have replaced with a fully functioning, indiscernible implant.'

Mayla jerked her hands up to feel her face. Her eyes stung with the beginning of tears, but she only felt the tears flowing across her right cheek.

'Be assured,' said Devin. 'Your face is as it was when you fell asleep.' She felt his cool hand on her forehead. 'I will show you as soon as you can move to the mirror.'

'What else?'

'Ovaries.'

Mayla wrenched her hands over to rest on her abdomen, feeling for scars. There were fine straight ridges on her belly. She coughed and drew in a deep breath. 'You said we were like the dead. How could parts of me be of any use?'

'The scientists of the New Eden project, experimented. It wasn't always successful. Often when the flesh was removed from the quantum connection with the sleeper it became part of this world again, revived. The drive for life is strong. They bathed the ovaries in a hormone rich formula and, in some cases, they became viable. Many sleepers made...donations.'

'Records state fertility rates in the remaining population had dropped to non-sustainable levels,' said Remi.

'It was speculated that the Earth had somehow curbed reproduction to aid the rebalancing, but the human desire for family was strong, so eggs were harvested and sold.'

'My eggs?' *This can't have happened.*

'Records—'

'Remi, enough.'

'You had children, Mayla. Others had them for you, your descendants would have lived perhaps reproduced. There are only small pockets of population now compared to when you fell asleep, but you may have family to discover. We can help you in the search if you choose.'

'They mutilated me.' She gagged and retched, tasting a sour version of the tea rising in her throat.

'You are safe.'

'Shut up!' Mayla screamed. 'How the fuck can you say I'm safe?'

'You were saved.' Devin cooed and gently wiped away her vomit and tears. 'After the exploitation of the Eden Project was discovered, you were saved from them. The corporations that survived accepted responsibility for the environmental damage they had caused. They set about righting their wrongs. Once they had discovered the violations being done, they rescued the sleepers.'

'What happened?'

'The corporations created the burrows and placed us with each sleeper. Assigned us to you … to be your carers.'

'Who are you?'

'We are—'

'I have a new reading,' ticked Remi. 'Second pulse trace.'

'A what? Pulse? What have they done to me?'

Everything went quiet, just whirring and then a slight rhythmic flicker of sound. 'It was a long time ago,' said Devin, 'but what do you remember, Mayla, about before you fell asleep?'

'It wasn't a long time ago,' she stammered. 'For me it was yesterday. I remember my life, my work, friends—'

'A male companion?'

'Michael. Why? Is he a sleeper? Did you find him too?'

'Checking Zone Control,' said Remi. He clicked. 'No records noting a name of Michael.'

That's why he wasn't here when I woke. Mind spinning. *How had it been for him? Did he find me? We had planned to meet that day. A picnic.*

She groaned and sobbed for her life wrenched away.

Yesterday I was in love. Today I'm alone. Violated. Mutilated.

Her world had vanished as she slept.

'The trace is faint.' Remi ticked on as though he was just reading random data to himself. 'An embryo, developing in normal pattern in line with five days post-implantation.'

'Michael is dead then?' she sobbed. 'Dead long ago.'

'There are many un-named sleepers,' said Devin. 'We can trace Zone Control records with DNA.'

'How?'

'Michael was your companion before you slept. Were you sexually intimate?'

'Why? Yes.'

'You had no sexual interaction others?' asked Remi.

'What are you talking about?'

'The bio-bed scans have discovered a very faint trace of life. It would seem that before you fell asleep you became pregnant.'

'You said they ... whoever, mutilated me, took my ovaries.' She breathed in sobbing chunks. Everything gone. Nothing made sense.

'We've seen the scans ... there is no doubt the harvest happened.' Devin stroked her shoulder with his cool, comforting hand.

'How can there be a baby?'

'It would have been barely implanted when you fell asleep. You would have had no clue. And when the harvesting happened the embryo was burrowed deep, microscopic and protected inside you. As you have been waking, it has awoken and continued to develop.'

'Development corresponding with eleven days of human embryonic growth,' clicked Remi.

'So, this is Michael's child? They didn't ... make me pregnant while I slept?'

'This baby started before you slept, so only you know the father,' Devin said.

'Michael's baby.' Mayla cupped her hands over her belly and wept. A universe of change between one eye-blink and the next.

'What do I do now?'

'Eat, rest, grow strong,' said Devin.

'We will monitor, supplement oestrogen,' said Remi.

'You aren't the only sleeper waking,' said Devin. 'Many borrows have signalled Zone Control that the sleepers are returning to their lives. It would be better for them to be welcomed back by their own kind.'

'Their own kind?'

Devin's cool arm slipped under Mayla's shoulder and he lifted her supporting her as she sat, blinking and willing her eyes to focus.

'We are charged with caring for sleepers in numerous burrows. If they all start waking at once, some will be left without anyone to say good morning to them. We would ask you to learn about the waking and help welcome the sleepers, your people, back into the world.'

'Of course. I'll do what I can,' said Mayla. She shivered as the last of the burning faded.

'Sensors indicate the waking process has successfully completed.' Remi made rattling noises in the gloom at the edge of the light. 'There was some whirring and a shiny tray appeared in the circle of light, followed by a shiny face. 'Are you ready for break-fast, Mayla.' Shiny face—shiny hands—wheels. Mayla flushed dizzy and hot, wobbled and was held safe by Devin's cool arms.

'You are safe, Mayla.' She blinked and focused on Devin's tanned face as he smiled a perfect smile. The white jacket—two buttons undone, showing where the thoroughly convincing approximation of perfect skin stopped and the shine began. Below the jacket—wheels.

Something inside Remi whirred as he placed the food in front of Mayla. 'The foetal DNA trace has been sourced.'

'Is the baby alright?'

'The baby is fine. The bio-bed has recorded its DNA. That information can be sent for matching to other burrows across world-wide network.'

Mayla watched the sleeper's eyelids flicker between dream and waking.

'Good morning,' she whispered. Her baby squirming, restless in her belly.

'Good morning, Michael.' A tear rolled down her right cheek. 'I'm glad you're here.'

2

Mile High

'There's a life sign in the waste pod,' said Joe as he switched on the pod camera.

'Well, yeah,' said Norris. 'Garbage men, sorry. Waste monitors have heart beats too.'

'Well, no. The pod doors are sealed and the cycle has started. No one should be in there.'

'Very bad for your health.' Norris pressed the alarm button.

Images from the waste pod wobbled and became solid on Joe's monitor. 'There's someone in there all right. A female shaped someone.'

Joe and Norris both turned towards the door as they heard the distinct clatter of Sally from sector security enter the control room. She wore archaic weaponry on a belt that rattled as she walked. A pistol and Taser jangled against antique hand-cuffs. They were so last century and no one in the right mind would use either weapon on Mile High. No one wanted any pesky holes shot through the walls and membranes they all relied on for staying alive. Air was thin and cold a mile up and punctured dirigibles tended to make rude noises as they deflated and fell out of the sky. It was already risky enough that the city council let any tattered old airship that could make it to Mile High tether and join the city, without someone shooting holes all over the place.

No one was all that worried that Sally would shoot at any one. There weren't any real crimes committed in Mile High, unless you count Sally's crime against fashion and good sense, but Joe liked how she looked all the same. No, there was only one penalty for a crime in the floating city and that was to strip the offender of their citizenship. Then they had to leave; walk the plank. So far it had proved a perfect deterrent.

'So, what's happening?' Sally asked as she leaned over Joe to get a look at the screen.

Joe could feel the cold metal of her pistol pressing into his back and something warmer and softer press into his shoulder. Some days being a garbage guy was great. 'Someone's in there.'

'So?' said Sally

'So, once the door is closed, the cycle starts automatically,' said Joe. 'She has about twenty-one minutes before she drops out when the floor opens to damp the rubbish.'

'Grizzly but not incorrect,' said Norris. 'Unless she can knit a parachute out of the trash in the pod in twenty minutes, then she won't be alive to experience the waste-land wonders of the down under.'

'Twenty minutes and she'll fall.' Sally leaned in again. 'You've got to be able to stop the cycle?'

'No,' stammered Joe. He struggled to concentrate on anything but the warm softness.

'So someone in Mile High is sending people to their death.' Sally stuck her thumbs into her weapon belt and turned to Norris. 'Who has clearance to start that cycle?'

'I'll get the names,' said Norris, leaving the control room.

Sally leaned into Joe's shoulder again. 'Damn,' he mumbled.

'Damn what?'

'Um, damn I wish she'd turn around so I could see who she is.'

The figure on the screen was definitely female and standing, staring at the digits on the outer door's panel that were slowly counting down the remaining, now eighteen, minutes of the pod cycle and her life. She just stood there frozen, except for the occasional swaying nudge caused by the linked dirigibles, of the floating city, bumping against each other as they travelled. Joe had well developed air legs, so he never noticed the nudging. He rarely noticed the city's movements but, while he watched her sway, he could feel every minute jolt.

'Why isn't she panicking?' said Joe. 'I sure would be.'

'It's not making sense,' said Sally. 'I know all the trouble makers in this cluster. I'd recognise her if she was one of them, so who would have a motive to kill her?'

'You're sounding like you fell out of an old movie.'

'Give a girl a break.' She punched him on the shoulder. 'Old detective movies are the closest thing I get to action in this drifting utopia.'

I'd help you find some action. Joe smiled to himself. 'Well Sally, what do they say? Don't do the crime coz you'd never survive the climb ... down that is.'

'I know. The idea of having to walk the plank is quite a deterrent.'

'If the only crime you see is in the old movies, why haven't you hung up your gun belt?'

'Good thing I didn't because someone did *do the crime* but now she will be doing the *climb*. You really can't open the door?'

'No.' Joe sighed and wiped beads of sweat from his top lip.

Sally walked over to look through the small window in the garbage pod door. 'There's no sign of a scuffle. She's not tied up. She just seems to be waiting, accepting it.' She shook her head.

'Shouldn't there be more yelling or crying?' Joe stood and walked over to stand close to Sally. 'She's about to fall to her death and she's just staring at the countdown.'

'Sixteen minutes to go,' Sally whispered and shuddered. 'We're looking at a murder being committed.'

'You okay?' Joe reached his hands out, gripping Sally's shoulders and pulling her towards him.

'I don't know how much good this list will be, there's lots of names,' said Norris, interrupting the moment.

Sally turned, pulling away from Joe's attempted comfort. 'Doesn't matter much unless someone on the list can halt the dump-cycle.' She took the list and scanned it. 'You two are on here. Where were you guys about fifteen minutes ago?'

'We're garbage guys,' said Joe. 'The trash doesn't come to us you know. We were doing a pick-up round.'

Norris nodded. 'Joe noticed the sensor as soon as we got back here.'

'And the others on the list?'

'Most of these are off shift.' Joe took hold of the list, and Sally's hand. Then crossed off the names of those who were off shift hours ago.

'Fourteen minutes,' said Norris.

'I'm afraid her fate is as sealed as the pod door, but I still need to find out who coded the door closed in case they decide to do it to someone else.' Sally sighed deeply.

'The system will have a record of the code,' said Joe. 'But I don't have clearance to—'

'The codes! Thank you.' Sally kissed Joe hard on the mouth. 'I am embarrassingly out of practice at solving crimes. I forgot that the system allocates everyone with an individual passcode.'

'Do you have access to them?' Joe gasped, his heart hammering.

Sally nodded and ran for the door, then stopped. 'Hey Norris, double check location logs to see where everyone on that list is, can you?'

'On it.'

'And Joe, can you ask coms why she might be wearing those ear buds. And that's not a personal sound cube she's holding.'

Joe looked through the small window at the girl's profile, now he could see, she was wearing tiny ear buds and holding some jerry-rigged bundle of wires. 'Good spotting.'

'That's what detectives do.' Sally gave a crooked, hopeful smile and disappeared.

Joe sent a request message to coms about the ear buds and then helped Norris firm up the locations of everyone on the garbage list. 'Eleven minutes.'

'We're one short,' said Norris. 'Double check me.'

'You're right, one short. Olga.' Joe flicked the duty screen on. 'She's off shift, but not lodged in to her quarters or in anyone else's.' He winked.

'I'll get someone in the Lookout to watch for her.' Norris messaged across to the Lookout in the central drift cluster, where off duty workers usually gathered to drink and relax.

'Seven minutes,' said Joe.

'I've got a password and a name,' said Sally, bursting into the control room.

'Let me guess,' said Joe. 'Your person is Olga.'

'Yep.'

'I have word from the Lookout,' said Norris. 'It appears our Olga is standing, pressed up against the side widow, staring out and has been for about twenty minutes.'

'How long does it take to walk from here to there?' asked Sally.

Joe smirked. 'Less than ten minutes.'

'Nate in coms has replied about the ear buds,' said Norris. 'Weird, but I'll read what he says, "She is wearing buds because she is Milly, and that's what she always does." He's coming up.'

Nate appeared in the doorway and stared at the swaying figure in the trash pod. 'That's her, Milly. She's from coms, but in another drift cluster. She transferred a couple of weeks ago and has worn the ear buds almost all the time since she arrived. She likes to tinker with the dodgy old comlinks.'

'She's still has one with her.'

'Do you know what she's listening to?' asked Sally.

'I thought she was chatting with that strange pale girl she spends time with, who never talks to anyone else. It didn't seem to stop her working so I ignored it.'

'Sounds like Olga,' said Sally.

'That's the name,' said Nate.

'What, Olga locked her in and is taunting her via some cobbled com-link while she waits for her to die?' said Joe.

'Why would she do that if they're friends?' asked Norris.

'Jealously? Maybe Milly was using the radio to whisper sweet nothings to Olga's fella.' Joe laughed. 'Just like in the old movies.'

'Five minutes.' Norris shook his head.

Nate stared at his shoes and held a head-phone tightly to one ear as the scanner searched each frequency. He looked back at Sally. 'She's listening to an external signal.'

'What!'

'Someone down under is talking to her.'

'More questions than answers.' Sally rubbed her temples. 'Why did this Olga want Milly in a garbage pod? And how did she force her to get inside?'

'I didn't. Hey, go easy, you gorilla.'

They turned and saw a broad shouldered, Lookout bouncer, shoving a small, sullen faced woman through the door. 'You must be Olga,' said Sally. Olga nodded stiffly and yanked her arm free of the bouncer.

'Three minutes.' Norris mumbled through his teeth.

'The passcode log shows that you started the pod cycle.' Another stiff nod. 'Why?'

'She begged me to.'

'Crap,' said Sally. 'You're saying she asked you to help her kill herself, and you said yes?'

'Nope, weirder … she wants to leave.'

'You're joking,' said Joe.

'Does this look like a comedy face to you? Look, I really want to go back to the window, so I can see if she makes it. Then you can charge me and make me walk the plank. I just want to see if it was all bullshit.'

'If what's bullshit?' asked Sally.

'I've known Milly since school, back on the starboard drift cluster. She always liked the com stuff. She had this hobby, building devices, and then she got curious to hear if there were any signals coming from down under. Then she heard … met Thomas and, I don't get it, but they seem to have fallen in love.' She shrugged. 'I reminded her what things were supposed to be like down low, but she believes what he's told her, and she decided to switch teams to be with him.'

'Well, there isn't going to be much of a romantic moment once the pod opens,' said Sally.

'This Thomas said he'd be waiting for her with some gear to soften her landing.'

'Right,' scoffed Norris. 'Mile High has a random trajectory. It stops all the trashy down low folk knowing where we'll be and trying to attack us.'

'It's all random except for one place.'

'Crossing the mountains,' mumbled Nate as he put the headphones down. 'Because of some of the old, smaller airships that have joined the city, we can only go so high. There is only one place we can traverse this mountain range. One non-random location. Sometimes we barely clear it by five decimetres.'

'And them down there know about it?' Norris shook his head.

'They're not stupid,' said Olga.

'So this Thomas knew when we'd be passing?'

'No, but he knew we would. He just watched out for us and told Milly when we were close.' Olga walked over and lightly touched her friend's image on the screen. 'That's when she asked for my help.'

There was a creaking screech as the floor began to slide open. Joe and Sally pushed their faces close to the tiny window. They could see patches of blue in places where the rubbish had already fallen away. Then they saw Milly smiling as she dropped from sight.

3

Finders-Keepers

Oh what a sad tale this might be. A tale of a child who wandered off from its parents at the seaside. While those parents were too busy with their own good times to watch the little one, it toddled out into the sea. Water up to its amazing little knees, a few more toddles, and the water was up to its chin. Then in a splash, up to its eyebrows. Oh, how the child did paddle and struggle alone in the deepening water.

But one of us was watching, and from below, we see the child, all floppy and drifting, sinking down from the brightest above. Now we have a choice to make. For you see, our kind have gills to get air and life from the water. We swim like a flash of silver-tailed lightning, flicking our tails, flick-flick and scoop that poor drowned child into our arms. Then we need to decide. Do we puff air and life, puff-puff, into those blue lips and push air into those little lungs, puff-puff, and raise the child back up to the sunshine to gulp the warm air and squawk and scream for its parents?

We could choose to do that helpful saving of that child. Some of us do, but most of us would decide another thing altogether. There would be no puff-puff. We'd take that drowned child and hold it tightly in our arms and turn towards the deeps, spiralling down from the bright teals and turquois to the deepest, darkest blue-blacks of the ocean. But that is not the end for that child from above. Its life is not over, but changed, changed, changed.

That water-logged babe from the above would be taken to Pelagya, the wise sea-witch.

Once Pelagya holds that child in her arms, she will use her kindly magic to wash away all its memories, so that when it wakes in its new life, it won't be crying with fright for the drowning or pining for its neglectful parents. For that lucky found child, a great undersea adventure awaits.

Pelagya will cradle that drowned and precious sprat in her strong dark arms, for she has become as dark as the bottom of the ocean. She will send her crooning thoughts to the babe as the mer-folk have no air to make a lullaby song. The old sea-witch will slip a tiny bright-shiny silver bubble of strong magic into the still, so still, blue-lipped mouth. She will sway and rock and send songs of magic and of love with her thoughts and her heart.

There would be a tiny swallow as the magic moves down the babe's throat. Then a squirm as the magic reclaims the drowned child. Its skin will smooth to shining silver. Its little toes will be covered and hidden by luscious flappy fins just like any other mer-folksy, for that is what that child is now. Then Pelagya will offer the new little mer-babe to grow our dwindled number.

As the finder has given a new soul to add to the mer-folk pod, Pelagya will honour the ancient promise. The witch will exchange that little sprat for a bubble full of the strongest mer-magic. The finder will swallow that dark, sticky, bitter-bitter globule of magic down into their gullet as quick as a blink.

It is said that once that magical gobbet bursts open inside them, it burns for days and nights and days, as the mer-folksy changes and ascends. At the end of the burning and changing, if all goes well, that mer-folksy will crawl out onto the sand with their slick silver tails changed forever into walky legs and footsies where their fins once had been.

We hope you are now figuring, from this sad tale, that not all mer-folk are born in the deep below under the sea. Some of them were born above, but they tottered into the brine and struggled, and sank below. Then wise Pelagya magically turned their tottering legs into twisty-turning tails.

Through time and tide, those once walker babes live out their lives as good and happy mer-folk should, but some, deep in their beating hearts, have a hungry desire for the above. They love to sneak up-up, to feel the sun on their faces and frolic in the washy waves. They sit on the rocks and watch and pine, wanting to feel the sand between the toes.

They know the promise of the magical exchange because there are no secrets between the mer-folk, so they wait and watch. They might see a luckless child drifting down, and then they have to choose. Will they give the puff-puff and lift the sprat up or will they spiral it down to the deepest deeps? Do not grieve, either way that babe has a life.

So, parents, be eyeful of your young toddles, for the seaside is not the place for babes with footsy-toes to go adventuring all on their own, and the mer-folk love the game of Finders-Keepers.

4

Time and Again

The smoke alarm blared. 'Oh crap! The cake.' Stella sprinted downstairs to the kitchen. The oven timer was bleating. Lacy wisps of smoke curled from the oven. Shoving on the cooking-mitt, she opened the door. A plume of sugary smoke billowed into her face. 'Shit.' She grabbed the charred cake, dropped it into the sink. It hissed as she turned on the tap.

The screeching alarm continued. 'Shut up,' she screeched back and flapped a cookbook underneath it. When the noise stopped, she slumped to the floor. 'Stink, and no cake. Not the type of party I was going for.'

Stella had gone to a lot of trouble to arrange things so this party for Mel would happen. She'd loved spending time with Josh, helping him surprise his sister, which guaranteed he'd be there. Stella would have a whole evening to see what could happen between her and Josh. She laughed about giving herself a timeframe, but she wasn't going to use the shoes anymore. It had taken five weeks to get them off the last time. Each time she used them it took longer.

The apartment stunk. The cake lay steaming in the sink. Her feet tingled. 'It's all such a mess, but I won't cancel the party now.' Her feet itched.

The shoes were buried under piles of jumpers and old books in the bottom of her wardrobe. She dug into the heap. Her grandmother's journal slid onto her foot. She kicked it into the back of the cupboard. She'd already ignored the warnings that were written inside.

The shoes felt warm in her hands. She slipped them on and they tightened around her feet. 'Just once more,' she whispered. Hoping it wasn't a lie. She needed to make this party happen and see where things might go with Josh.

Stella stood, wriggled her toes, thought about the time not so long ago, when she was sliding the uncooked cake into the oven. She stepped and found herself bending over the open oven with a face full of heat. She slid the cake tin in, closed the door and set the timer. This time she sat at the kitchen table and picked up her book. The time passed, *again*. This time she heard the timer beep and the cake was done. Perfect.

While the cake cooled, Stella chopped cheese and arranged nibbles. The shoes were still firm and warm on her feet. She knew it would take a while for them to released her. She iced the cake and went down to the fridge in the garage to grab the bubbly.

Scruff-Ball liked to sleep on the third flight of stairs, and she flicked her tail at the absolute wrong moment. Stella stood on it. The cat screeched, twisted around and bit Stella. She dropped the case of wine bottles and watched them tumble and explode in a fizzing disaster.

It took thirty-three minutes for Stella to clean up the broken glass and mop the champagne off the stairs. Blood oozed from the cat-bite, and she'd cut her hand on some glass, but she had not used the shoes. She needed more champagne and some first aid. She closed her eyes and sighed. 'I need more time.' The shoes warmed, tightened, tingled.

Stella thought of the rattly old fridge downstairs. She stepped, pulled the fridge door open, *again.* Cool air flowed out as she lifted the case of champagne and headed upstairs.

'Hi, Scuff-Ball,' she said as she slowed and passed the cat on the third flight of stairs.

The shoes tightened as she rinsed the glasses. *'Retour - repeating an hour or a day, costs you and hour or a day,'* her grandmother had warned in her journal. *'Be careful what you choose to use your time on.'* Stella thought about spending time with Josh. 'Worth it.' She would try soaking the shoes off after the party.

Mel was surprised and delighted that her quiet birthday dinner had turned into a party. Stella was glad she'd stepped back and used up a couple of hours to make everything just right. Josh draped his arm around Stella's shoulder as he bragged about them surprising his sister. The complements and the cute jokes flowed between them, and Stella glowed. They danced. Josh helped serve the unburnt cake and chilled champagne. Later, they teamed up for tipsy karaoke duets, and guessed each other's goofy clues in charades. People were starting to say their goodbyes.

'You two are psychic,' said Jeff as he and Martin shrugged on their coats and squeezed Mel in one last birthday hug.

'Psychic. That's me,' Stella bragged.

'Okay.' Josh smiled. 'If you can guess my favourite movie, I'll help you clean up.'

'No problem.' Stella touched her fingers dramatically to her temples. 'Star Wars.'

Josh shook his head. 'Blade Runner.'

Stella was hot. The shoes squeezed. Her feet tingled. Step.

'If you can guess my favourite movie, I'll help you clean up.'

'No problem.' Stella touched her fingers dramatically to her temples. 'Blade Runner.'

'Wow! Yes.'

'Thank you so much for the surprise,' said Mel grabbing Stella and Josh into a hug. 'Now, I'm out of here because I'm *not* cleaning up.' The last stragglers laughed and nodded following Mel out the door. Stella and Josh were alone.

'Thanks for helping, Josh. Everything looks great.'

'You're welcome. And thanks for helping me surprise Mel.' He took her hands. 'I had a great time tonight.'

'Me too.' She squeezed his hands. He kissed her. Wonderful.

Her feet itched, the shoes tightened. She took a micro step.

Josh squeezed her hands *again*, kissed her *again*. The shoes loosened. Lifting her heals out, she felt cool air on her skin. She knew about this from the journal. The shoes were loosening because she wouldn't need them to have time with Josh.

But I have Josh—now. She chose, stepped, and kissed he again. The shoes tightened, her feet itched. She stepped back, again, kissing Josh again, and again and again.

5

One-Hundred Percent

Jade woke with her knee resting on her eye. Her lashes blinked and tickled the skin on that knee. Next she noticed the weight. She was curled and the weight of her legs pressed down on her chest, making it hard to breathe. Something sharp was sticking into the back of her throbbing head. Her curled weight was pressing her head onto this unknown something. Jade didn't know why any of these things were happening or when they had happened.

She had been reaching to pull the binoculars out of the cupboard. She had been smiling, happy to be doing a tower shift. A morning out of the sun and away from the chance of beach balls hitting her in the back of the head. She was one-hundred percent committed to surf lifesaving and even more in love with the beach, but watching from up in the tower was a pleasant break. It was also nice to be recognised for her experience and competence.

Jade opened her eyes. Blood trickled in, washing her vision red. Her hand reached behind her head towards the unknown something. It felt like the tower doorknob. Her hand came away bloody. Her head was against the door that was vertical moments ago. How long ago?

Outside, Jade could see water where it shouldn't be, flowing foamy, flattening the dune grasses as it washed toward the sea. As the water level dropped she saw the toilet block upside down and a little sideways. Nope. She was upside down and a little bit sideways, and confused, and scared.

She scrambled, pushed against the door. Forcing her legs out, kicking away the stool. It clattered against a window, which shattered, crackling into a sheet of wavering diamonds then sagging in the frame.

After clambering upright, Jade stared around at everything that was now wrong and broken. She and the tower station were only a metre above the ground instead of eight. The poles supporting the tower were bent like giant crumpled drinking straws. The stairs were twisted around them. The board rack was hanging from a bent pole by one bolt. Only one rescue board remained.

The pandanus trees that edged the picnic area at the top of the dunes were laying over. Their roots looked like claws ripped away as they failed to grip the ground. The straggly dune grass and the wire fences draped the row of fallen trees like eerie bunting.

Jade wrapped her towel around her hand and thumped at the sagging window. Glass fragments rained down onto the too-close ground. She flung her towel over the jagged window frame and scrambled outside.

All the smells of ice-cream and chips and sun screen had been drowned by the stench of fish and sewerage. Café tables dangled from the sagging guttering along the North Street shopfronts. The carpark was full of sand and cars piled against each other, topped with twisted sunshades, broken surfboards and deflated beach toys. All the tilted trees around the park were draped with towels and eskies.

The only thing missing were the people. Birds squawked, toilet pipes gurgled, things clunked and settled into their new positions, but there were no sounds of people. Then Jade heard a small cry for help. Not small, far off. Down at the beach.

She turned from destruction of the street and gasped. The beach had no waves, no glistening blue. The ocean had drawn away, revealing a sandy-rocky hill down into the valley that lay under the water between here and the island. Half way down the slope was a kid, screaming and hanging on to a very twisted leg, which was attached to a leg-rope and a busted board. Beyond the screaming kid, was the shadowy line of the second wave building way off in the east.

Jade grabbed the last rescue board from the twisted rack and ran out towards the kid, because she was one-hundred percent committed to surf lifesaving.

6

The Time Treader

Once upon a then and now, or perhaps it was a before or after, there was a traveller named Neenish Montgomery who had the knowledge and contrivances to travel to precise times and places and offer people well timed assistance. Neenish wasn't concerned about the plights of people in his past, his concern was to make a gainful deal.

It was almost harvest time in the farming district of Home Fires. Sheriff Milly Tooke was leaning on the railing outside her office, the mayor, August Redding and Tansy Nash, the leader of the town's Chamber of Commerce, leaned there with her. They were all smiling.

'It looks like it'll be a bumper crop this year,' Milly said, looking out across the fields at the tall stalks of corn swaying in the early morning breeze.

'It sure will be,' said Tansy. 'We've got better corn than any of the other districts this season. It'll bring the best prices at market.'

'We needed this,' said Mayor Redding. 'Folks in Home Fires work hard. They deserve prosperity.'

'This year will go down in the annals,' said Tansy. 'The town will talk about it for years.'

'So today's the big harvest day?' said Milly, pointing to the thin smudge of grey that skimmed the hills to the east. 'We should get everyone up and started early,' she said 'looks like there'll be storms later today.'

'Wet corn would be mouldy before it reaches the market.' Tansy shook her head.

'I'll send out a weather alert on the Vox and get harvesting started.' Mayor Redding stopped leaning and turned towards his office.

'It's not a storm that you're seeing on the horizon.' The voice from behind them was cool and unfamiliar. All three of them spun to look at the stranger. 'Good morning,' the cool voice said. 'I'm Neenish Montgomery.' The slim stranger lifted his hand. Sheriff Milly shook it. As did Tansy and August in turn.

'Of course it's a storm.' August Redding shook his head and smirked. 'Locals around here are skilled at reading the skies.'

'I read something else that told me that this specific smudge, on this specific day, is no storm.'

'What's else could it be, Mr Montgomery?' asked Milly.

'Something much worse.'

'What did you read? And who are you to be … appearing just like that with all your stories.' The mayor was beginning to bluster at the stranger.

'It's fine August,' said Tansy, laying a calming hand on the mayor's shoulder. 'Mr Montgomery is just a visitor and we want him to feel welcome in Home Fires.'

'Thank you, Tansy. Please call me Neenish.' Tansy gave a squeezed up smile, she was sure she hadn't offered the stranger her name.

'Tell us about yourself, Mr ... Neenish,' said Sheriff Milly. 'August could you go and send that message over the Vox. Let's get the harvest started.'

'It won't matter. Not unless you let me help you.'

'Help us with what?' asked Tansy.

'The locusts.' Neenish pointed at the long smear that was darkening on the distant hills.

'It can't be locusts.' Now, Mayor Redding smirked and rolled his eyes. 'Sir, you are not local, as we have established. If you were, you would know we had trouble with locusts three harvests back.' He huffed. 'Locusts have a seven-year cycle. They won't be back for four more harvests.'

'It is locusts. And locusts have no concept of years as you perceive them,' said Neenish. 'Send your drone up Sheriff, if you don't believe me.'

The drone went out to inspect the smudge. Milly, August and Tansy stared at the small screen. Neenish stood back, watching the darkness move closer to Home Fires and making adjustments to three or four of the five knobs protruding out around his oversized silver pocket-watch.

'It's locusts.' Sheriff Milly's voice was a choked whisper. 'Get onto the Vox now, August. We've got to get as much corn harvested as we can and get it inside the sheds.'

'Hungry locusts will find the cracks in your sheds,' said Neenish. 'But I can help you.'

'What can you do?' asked Milly.

'I can use this,' he held up his pocket-watch. 'to send them away to when they can't do any more harm.'

'Fool!' growled August. 'Are you insane?'

'I understand your scepticism. Might I offer a demonstration.' Neenish bowed his head and concentrated on twirling the knobs on his watch. 'Tansy, you had a loyal hound, Rufus, wasn't that his name?'

Tansy's eyes were suddenly glassy. She nodded silently.

'It was so sad. He was crushed by a dead branch falling from the tree that his favourite, shady napping spot.'

'How do you know about ...' Neenish touched his watched and flickered to nothingness. A moment later, he reappeared with a sleepy looking brown hound lolling in his arms.

'Rufus!' Tansy raced over and hugged the bleary eyed dog.

'How did you do that?' asked Mayor Redding.

'I'm a Time Treader.'

'A time *what*?' asked Milly.

'This device lets me travel through time to help people. I know when things happen, or will happen and I can help ... for a price.'

'So you can help get rid of the locusts?' Milly stared at the shining watch.

'I can.'

'And what do we have to pay you?' asked the Mayor.

'Half of the corn crop.'

'What! No, this is the best crop we've had for years,' blustered the mayor. 'It's the towns wealth. We have to think of Home Fires, the needs of the children. You have time-travel, what do you want with tonnes of corn?'

'The time I come from has amazing technologies ... and we need them, for we have neglected and destroyed much of the world. I'm obliged by my community to seek out resources and bring them up time or ...'

'Or what?'

'I have to think of children as well?' Neenish was quiet for a long moment, then he shook himself and stood tall. 'So, half the crop and I'll save the town. Do we have a deal?'

'Give us a moment to decide,' said Sheriff Milly, as she huddled close to the other two.

'Don't take too long,' said Neenish and he walked in the direction of darkening sky.

After a very short while, Milly announced, 'We agree.' The other two glared at her. 'We can negotiate after the crop is safe,' she whispered to them. 'We have no choice.'

'Go and send the Vox message, August,' said Tansy. 'Explain all this as best you can and wake people so they can see the miracle we are going to pay so much for.'

The sleepy folk of Homes Fires stumbled into the early morning light just in time to see the Neenish Montgomery standing at the eastern edge of the huge expanse of corn fields. He was watching the advancing cloud of locusts and adjusting his device. It buzzed and cast a huge vertical lasso of energy that stretched out and up between the corn fields and the locusts cloud.

The manifestation thrummed and glittered. The folk of Home Fires twitched. Their skin prickled and their hair stood on end. They watched and silently implored, that this stranger could do as he claimed.

As the energy swirled in the sky above the corn fields, the locusts changed directions funnelling towards the crackling loop above the time treader's head. The black buzzing cloud narrowed into a giant hungry arrow-head. It raced straight at the precious crops. 'No.' The whole town joined in the breathy, desperate whisper. 'No, no, no.'

The locusts reached the energy loop and as they crossed over into the fields, they were gone. The funnel of swarming black grew smaller and smaller at the edge of the precious crops until there was nothing but shimmering blue sky. The sparkling lasso folded in on itself and it too was gone. The time treader stowed his watch in his pocket and walked back towards the sheriff's office.

Everyone was cheering. 'I'm glad I could help,' said Neenish humbly. 'Now that everyone has been awakened, it's time to get to harvesting so that I can take my payment. The sheriff and the mayor shared a look of concern and turned toward Tansy, who glanced up as she spoke quietly with members of the Chamber of Commerce.

'Let's get the corn in,' said the mayor. 'Neenish, we have a busy day ahead, but please be our guest at dinner this evening and explain to us what you did to save our town.'

'I simply sent the locusts back in time to when they could do no damage,' said Neenish around a mouthful of corn-cakes, peas and chicken. 'Delicious.'

'How do you know for sure they were destroyed?' asked Milly. 'We couldn't live with the

notion of having caused other people this affliction'

'I know for sure because I know time, sheriff.'
Neenish smiled his all-will-be-well smile, pleased
that the deal had gone so smoothly. 'I know that
eons ago this valley was covered by the sea. Unless
I am wrong, locusts cannot breathe under water
any better than the good and wise folk of Home
Fires can fly.'

'So you're saying your device sent then into
the past where they drowned?'

'Every last hungry one of them, yes,' said
Neenish.

'And you can't bring them back?' asked Mayor
Redding, glancing over at Tansy who flashed a
look to the gathered associates of the Chamber of
Commerce.

'It would be possible, but I doubt you have
need for thousands of soggy insect corpses. Or do
you need proof before you pay me?' Neenish narrowed his gaze.

'Well,' stammered Tansy. 'We, the members of
the Chamber of Commerce ... the town would

like to renegotiate our original deal. Half the crop is a huge amount to give away, Mr Montgomery.'

'We had an agreement.' Neenish looked down at his half-finished meal. He thought of his family, up-time, and how different things were for them. They depended on him to make his tithe. He knew what could happen to them if he didn't send the corn. His voice had dropped to an icy whisper. 'I won't renegotiate. I can't.'

'Why should we pay him at all?' squawked the mayor. 'He said himself that the locusts are drowned. Even if he brought them back, we could shovel them onto the fields for fertilizer.'

'We need to save the town funds,' said one of the associates.

'For the children,' said another.

'Neenish, you have a powerful machine, you have access to the whole of time, go somewhere else and find a fortune.'

'Yes,' declared the chamber associates with unanimous conviction. 'We will keep the crops, and the money they bring, for the children.'

The wholesome dinner was sour in his mouth as Neenish forced himself to chew while he listened to the chamber of commerce's grand altruistic plan to rob him of his fee and save the funds for the future of the children. His face stiffened with silent rage.

He stood and spoke in reply to the mayor's argument. 'I had seen the tragic history of Homes Fires in our ancient books.' He spoke with quiet eloquence. 'I too thought of your children, and wept at the hunger and hardship they and you would suffer, because of this year's ruined crop, only a few short years after the last failed harvest, so I came. This harvest has been saved, but it was not so in your original timeline. I know, I've visited the museum libraries in my time and seen it in the ancient town almanacs. Because of my help Home Fires has been saved.' He drew a shuddering breath. 'We had our agreement.'

'We should honour the agreement,' argued Milly. 'We will get plenty of money from selling our half of the crop.'

'But it cost Neenish nothing to help us,' justified the mayor.

Neenish pulled his watch from his pocket and stared at it. 'Helping you has cost me time,' he said.

The mayor smiled and raised his arms, indicating around the gathered town folk. 'Do you have children, Neenish?'

'I do.'

'So you understand raising children takes time and effort. All of us have given our time freely for the good of the children, and we thank you for your generosity in giving some of your time for the good of our children.'

'I need ... the corn,' Neenish said.

'How about this?' The mayor's smile was stiff. 'Instead of corn, we offer you the generosity of our town for as long as you wish to stay.'

'I must have my payment.' His words were barely a breath.

'As I said, Mr Montgomery, you are welcome to whatever Home Fires has to offer.'

'So that is our new deal?' said Neenish, 'For me to take what your town has to offer? And make use of it for as long as I like?'

'Certainly.' The mayor clapped Neenish on the back and strode away towards his mayoral villa.

Warm light, muffled chatter and supper-time laughter flowed from windows around town as Neenish walked to the guest cottage which had been prepared for him. As he walked he made his plans to take what the fair town of Home Fires had to offer as payment for saving their crops from the locusts.

The cool quiet of early morning was pierced by urgent talk. The voices raised and spread from home to home. Then the urgent voices called names. The names of the children. The called names became shouts of panic. Except for a few squalling babes, the children of Home Fires where nowhere to be found. Neenish heard the ruckus and stepped into the cool of the morning to clarify the details of the new deal the mayor had made with him last evening.

Milly came running up the Neenish. 'All the kids are gone,' she said. 'Where are they?'

'They're here ... in Home Fires.' Neenish glance at his watch.

'Where?' boomed the mayor as he rushed up close to Neenish. 'The town's in an uproar. You better give me answers before people come asking what you did.'

'Where are they, Neenish?' Milly asked again.

Neenish turned and started walking. 'I'll show you.'

'The kids? You did this didn't you,' said Tansy, leading a trail of associates behind here.

'How did you guess?' Neenish offered a sad smirk.

'Because I can't find Rufus anywhere,' said Tansy.

'I sent him back. Maybe he will decide to sleep under his favourite tree again, maybe not,' said Neenish quietly. 'Search your thoughts for a moment... see what new memories you have there now?'

Tansy stopped, and focused inward. Tears rolled down her cheeks. 'You sent him back knowing he could die.'

Mayor Redding grabbed Neenish by the shoulder. 'I demand you show us where our children are.'

'They are here.' Neenish gestured towards the graveyard.

'Where, Mr Montgomery? Explain yourself,' blustered the mayor.

'Oh no. You couldn't have,' said Milly.

'I didn't harm them. They all died of old age.' He stepped into a cluster of weathered tombstones that had not been in the Home Fires graveyard the day before. 'I needed corn. It was vital that I bring the corn up-time. It was needed very badly. The consequences would have been ...'

'So you took our children instead,' bellowed the mayor. 'How could you exchange our children for corn. Arrest him.' Neenish vanished.

Over the next few minutes, the town's people gathered and wept in an ever growing chain of sadness as the inconceivable details of the time treader's payment was realised. When Neenish appeared again he was looking out from a small window, high-up in the chapel. People ran at the locked door. He rattled the chapel keys out of the window.

'I needed the corn,' Neenish said. 'My family, my town, in my time, needed the corn. I didn't harm your children.'

'I don't understand,' said Milly.

'There is always a payment to reckon. I let you decide what you could afford. You agreed you would give the corn.' Neenish was weeping. 'When you refused ... I took your children. They knew how to grow the corn. It was hard work starting out with new ground. All the ploughing, building shelters ... I did what I could to ease their toil. You would be proud of them. You should be proud of them ... they built this town for you.'

'You sent them back in time to farm your corn?' Milly's face was wet with tears.

'You could have bought them back when they had finished,' said Tansy.

'The mayor said I could take what your town had to offer and make use of it for as long as I liked.' Neenish wiped his tears on his sleeve. 'There was nothing I liked about what I did, but I needed the corn, and it took many, many years to grow as much as you had in half of this single year's harvest. Your children were happy enough. They lived long lives.' Neenish pointed to the weather aged gravestones, etched with the names of so many children that were to be Homes Fire's future, who were now it's past. Then he vanished.

7

Lady Luck

Luck is delicious. It tastes of dreams and optimism. Tantalising vapours rise from the hopeful humans all around me. I flit and glide between them, feeling giddy at the promise of feasting on all the elation radiating from them. They are flesh-bound luck factories.

They believe luck comes from somewhere outside themselves, some mystical other place, effecting how the next ball drops, influencing the roll of the dice, or making the flashing full house appear on the screen with the next coin they drop into the machine. They won't let themselves see that they weave their own luck - or otherwise - from the choices they make.

They wait, breath held, fingers crossed, silent deals made to whichever higher power. The air is thick with dreams. They're all so certain the big break is just a jumpy heartbeat away. With a nod, I can give them a small win, then joy bubbles out through their skin, flowing vaporous across their bodies. I can smell it. I can see the sparks. I glide in close. Nibbling, licking—delicious.

Sometimes, the coins don't drop, or the horse runs slowly, or the dice rolls bad. Then there's doubt, pessimism - that can lead to second thoughts. So I do my bit to keep the delicious optimism seeping. I'm not so insubstantial, you know. I can nudge those dice, or whisper in the horse's ear, do a sneaky shuffle of the cards. I can even squirm inside the electrical innards of those coin-stealing, hope-stealing machines and make some static to change their cold electric minds, causing the coins to drop. And with every little win, glee oozes from each human player.

With or without the luck, they are feeling what I know. That hope is tantalising. So I hunt out the fleetingly fortunate. I harvest what they fritter away and feast on it.

I follow a human, reeking of hopeful dreams and misplaced optimism. I hover just above his shoulder, and drink in the heady vapours that waft up with each little win.

I can barely stand waiting, but it won't be long now. His luck is fraying, coming lose. He's almost used up the last of today's dreams of winning. But he still believes his luck will change. And it could, it will, because that's his choice.

I stop my tinkering. The pock-pock of doubt takes over as the winning stops. As the last coin disappears into the machine, his succulent, delicious luck is flapping all around him, lifting and floating free. I drift up from his shoulder, twirling, wrapping myself in the exquisite gossamer spun from this human's hopes and dreams. I devour the luck as I rise.

I will call on this one again, when his addiction and mine need to be satisfied.

Luck is delicious.

8

The Weed

'I found info-fragments in the ancient records,' said the red-faced pundit. 'It's just a condition, some form of syndrome.'

'What is?' Rapunzel huffed.

'The way you feel about ... Aunt Witch. That you miss her and miss the tower...being imprisoned up there.'

'It was a sanctuary, not a prison. If it wasn't for Aunt Witch, who knows what would have happened to me.' Rapunzel squeezed her hands into fists.

'She took you from your parents. You were just an infant, crying for your mother's breast.'

'Aunt Witch wasn't stealing. She was testing them. Testing to see if my mother could think about anything except the weed. She loved it so much she named me after it.' Rapunzel stood and moved to the window, staring out towards her tower in the distance. 'Aunt Witch told my mother she could help herself to all the Rapunzel weed in her garden if she would trade the child as payment. When mother heard the deal, she couldn't shove me into Aunt Witch's arms fast enough.'

'Your mother was suffering from an affliction,' the pundit stuttered his excuses.

'Aunt Witch saw her *affliction*. She saw my mother neglecting me. She saw my father cowering as my mother fretted and raged, needing more and more weed. So she took me.'

'She locked you in a tower.' The pundit spluttered.

'It seems you have thorns in your eyes. Can't you see what the Aunt Witch did for me, for all the girls you claim she has taken?' Rapunzel's gaze was soft and far away. 'She made sure we were safe and loved. She took herbs to conjured milk from her breast so she could suckle us. We were taught to read and write, to create music and fine crafts. We sisters studied and reasoned. Aunt Witch saw our value and our uniqueness.'

'She wouldn't let you down from your tower. There was no way out for you.'

'And there was no way for harm to come in...until you sent that charming beguiler to make me believe Aunt Witch was dying. Your false hero promised to take me to her.'

'It was necessary. He has a magical knack.' The pundit puffed his chest proudly. 'Not one of the girls in the towers resisted his princely charm.'

'He convinced me to cut off my hair.' Tears flowed as she stared at her cropped hair in the window's reflection. 'I nailed my braid to the window sill and climbed down. Then he set my tresses on fire.' She sobbed. 'He tricked me and burned my only way home.' Rapunzel thumped her fist on the pundit's desk. 'You captured the only family I've ever known, and you say I have a syndrome and there's something wrong with me.'

'Your mother and father were heartbroken about what they did. They want to see you.'

'I want to see Aunt Witch. I miss her.'

'She is on trial, but you are welcome at your parent's home.'

'Are the other girls agreeing to return home?'

The pundit stared at the floor.

'They aren't, are they?' Rapunzel stared out across the town that had never been her home. In the courtyard below was a small windowless brick cell with a heavy bar across the door. Outside the door a broom leaned against the block wall. Rapunzel knew every knot in that broom stick. It was her way home. 'My sisters are all here, aren't they?'

The pundit nodded his head slowly. 'We hoped we could get through to you, reason with you.'

'Aunt Witch saved me. She saved us all. Now we will repay her kindness.' Rapunzel shoved the pundit backward, toppling him and his chair. He lay like a turtle stranded on its back. Rapunzel pushed through the heavy wooden door. The sound of cheers and doors slamming open echoed up through the spiral staircase as she descended.

'No matter what had been expounded from the old records, it's not a syndrome,' mumbled the pundit as he grunted and stood up. 'Not at all.' He powered down his journal and replaced his stylus into its housing. Looking out the window, he saw Rapunzel and her sisters freeing Aunt Witch from the cell and placing the broom in her hands. It was the way home for all of them.

9

Rong

Night was falling above, the water felt thicker to swim through as it cooled. Each tail-thrust te made flicked up swirls of silt-darkened sand, making hunting difficult. It was hard enough hunting alone, without pod-mates to herd the fish and swirl them until they were disoriented and easy to capture. Catching food alone relied on stealth and speed.

Sonic chitters from the fish made sound trails through the water. Flexing ter powerful tale, te turned, honing in on the sounds made by the food. Gliding round a rocky outcrop, the fish came into sight. Te crouched ready. Legs pushed against the rock, tail flicked. Te plunged through the shoal, grasping one fish in each hand, ter thumbs jamming deep into the gill slits to be sure the fish couldn't wriggle lose and escape.

The fish flicked and twisted to be free of their captor. Terrified chitters and neumes flowed through the water blasting into ter mind. This close, the intensity of the panic signals coming from the captured fish hurt. A deep bite into each twisting fish ended their fear and the painful neumes. Te drifted watching the thin ribbons of blood trail away on the current. Holding the food fish with reverence, te quieted.

I offer thanks to Mother Ocean for being the giver of all life. As the neume of thanks was sent out through the water, ter sunk down into the tall seaweed to feed.

Sated, te bobbed in the current, resting, tail coiled into twists of thick kelp to stop from drifting. Because of many hungry days alone, te always made sure to share the good fortune of a hunt. Letting go of the fish heads, te watched as they sank through the water coming to rest on the silty sand. Crabs sauntered in, fighting over the ragged pieces of flesh on the heads. The kelp swayed, this was a good place to sleep. Te coiled into a protective curve and let ter eyes closed. Rocked into sleep by Mother Ocean.

Waves of pain flooded into ter's mind. Awake, alert, tensed to swim from danger, then relaxing as the pain signal defined itself. Fear, layered with physical pain, blasting through the water. This neume felt unfamiliar, but the message was clear. A creature was in grave trouble. It was alone, frightened, in pain. Te would never leave another alone to suffer.

Untwining from the kelp, te glided into the dark water following this peculiar neume. Darkness was everywhere, the neume was the only trail to rely on. The mind sending this signal remained a mystery. Ahead, the blackness lightened. An orb of light, like the glow of the deep ocean dwellers. But this light jolted frantically. A beam of brightness casting twisting knots of shadow through the thick kelp. *Panic*—the creature was tangled. Creatures only tangle on purpose, to hide, to rest, but this one struggled and the weed clung, trapping it.

The creature's neumes weakened. The light twisted more slowly. The neumes became bursts of colour, fading into a deepening blackness. Heavy heat inside it, like time spent too close to the lava vents in the deeps. Heart slowing, like a food fish after it's bitten.

Pushing against the thick kelp, te followed the now still glow into the tangle. At first this slick, glowing creature made no sense. Pulling it free of the tangles, the awareness flooded in. This was a walker, from above.

Walkers had swimming skins so they could venture into the below and survive with no gill or fin. Mother Ocean's creatures could persist in the sea with fin or gill, but never neither. Cautious, te crouched, tail braced and pushed off, as if hunting. Grasping the walker around its black-skinned body, te pushed them both up towards the moon-flecked surface of the water.

Once its head came above the water, the walker's mind shrieked painful waves of panic as it honked out ragged breaths. Its body jolted and heaved, making it difficult to hold afloat. It pushed the tools off its face and they floated away. The fading mind signals throbbed into dark swirls of confusion. *Sad—relief—fatigue.* It floated limp in ter arms, it's breath calming. It signalled—*gratitude.*

'Thank you,' it said.

Te took a breath, feeling the cool night air tickle through ter gills. 'Good?' Te tried the questioning tone te'd heard walkers use.

'Yeah, I'm good,' it said.

Te hadn't known how to *talk*, how to piece together the walker words as they did so easily. For a long time, te had listened from afar, matching the walker air words with their neumed mind signals, but te didn't know how to begin.

'My gear's on the beach.' The walker gestured towards a small shelter on the sand. It twisted away and swam for the shore, neuming, *gratitude— happiness—pod-bond.* Te's heart raced at the feeling of welcome and belonging this walker was signalling. Te followed until ter feet touch bottom and ter tail scraped on the sand.

The walker turned. 'I'm Ash. Thank you. You saved me.'

'Night swimming unsafe. Why?'

'I was curious about animal activity at night. It's my work to do surveys of the tidal zones.' *Care—heart-bond—protection.* 'This place is beautiful, precious. The time I spend here is peaceful, and I'm away from my family drama. I decided to go into deeper, unfamiliar water. I know I shouldn't have been diving alone.'

'Alone is bad.'

'Tell me about it.' Ash stepped inside its shelter. Te felt neumes of aloneness from it.

'I would yes... tell you about it.' Te had a sudden gnawing need to share, to not be alone. Rejection had been life-long, te could not get more alone, and the idea of being less alone was tantalising.

Te took slow steps up the beach. Squatting in the shadows next to the shelter, next to where the dark swimming skin lay twisted on the sand. The shelter jostled and Ash came out covered in a more familiar lose fitting skin the colour of reef fish.

'Are you cold? Do you want a fire?' asked Ash.

'Not cold.'

'Do you want something a drink, fruit?'

The neume signal made some sense. Drink, purposeful placement of water into self. Strange, but the offer of shared nourishment was elating. 'Fruit.' Te neumed, *gratitude*, hoping the signal would make up for the lack of ter word knowledge.

Ash offered a stumpy eel shaped fruit. Then took one for itself and pulled off the skin. Te copied the movement. Copied again placing the blind eel flesh into ter mouth. This was non-prey, there was no panic neume or end to life as te bit into it. It was - a foraged food. It did not taste of the sea. The sharp lack of salt stung with tingling strangeness. Liquid filled ter mouth and overflowed, flowing down.

'Tastes that good?'

'Good,' te said around the fruit, swallowing the slippery lump. 'Thank you.'

The moon came out from behind a cloud. 'You've got a tail. What the fuck!' Te's mind swam with Ash's flood of signals. *Shock—fear—disbe-*

lief—fear. Many question tones, blurred together like the panic neumes captured food fish.

Te neumed and spoke. 'You safe, like pod.' Ash's panic sored. Its heart pounded. Te wanted to ease Ash's panic and could easily. Ter kind, the Abrax, had neumes with extremely strong influence. Pod members had used these types of neumes on ter as a youngling, to force ter to make life ending choices and rid their pod of the two-legged monster. Te did not believe in using control neumes. The invasion had left spirit wounds te never wanted to inflict on another, but as Ash's distress surged again, te neumed a tide of thoughts to soothe. *Calm—safe—pod-bond—safe—calm.* And released the control quickly. 'Safe.'

'Safe,' Ash repeated. 'Like pod. What the fuck does that mean? What are you?'

Te very slowly stood, stepped away from Ash to show no danger and froze in place. Sending neumes to cast a pictures. *Pod-mates—other pods of Abrax—young and old—hunting—swimming—ceremony.* 'From mother-ocean,' te said.

'From the ocean,' Ash stuttered. 'Like a mer...' Its neume showed images of creatures swimming, twisting around coral reefs.

'Yes ... mer, no...Abrax.' Te placed a hand on terself then gestured out across the dark water.

'Abrax. From the ocean. But, you have legs.'

'Not Abrax ... me alone.' Te neumed the mistake that was ter form, the shame and the unbelonging of exile from pod-mates, from all Abrax.

The neumes continued until Ash mumbled, 'Wrong.' It shook its head. 'Your people say having legs is wrong.'

'Rong is me. It is Ash, I am Rong.'

'Your *pod* named you wrong?'

Te nodded. 'I am Rong. I not stay with Abrax. Belong alone, or walker?' Rong pointed to Ash's legs and signalled about the times te had wondered about the possibility of belonging among the walkers. The neume overflowed with frustration and loneliness that had always accompanied the wondering. 'I go back.' Te looked out across the dark water.

'No.' Ash stood, stepped forward and took Rong's hand. 'Don't go. You're amazing, you saved me, that's wonderful.' Ash's neume, *gratitude – acceptance*, washed through Rong with such force ter legs buckled.

Ash reached to hold Rong steady, then tripped over Rong's tail and they fell together onto the stiff ground covering laid over the sand.

'Forgive,' Rong stammered.

Ash, started making deep huffing sounds and neumed, *delight—happiness*. It continued to huff, then calmed its breath. 'Sorry. I'm not laughing at you. It's not every day you find yourself laying on the sand with a naked ... what are you?'

'Abrax.'

Ash laughed again and they helped each other to sit up. 'I'm mean... gender. I was about to say, rolling around with a strange man, but ... well—' Rong felt the question in Ash's neume.

'Proliferation. I am neither until it is my time. I will be egg bringer or seed bringer.'

'You're neither gender, sorry, egg or seed? And then you are one or the other?'

'For proliferation. At that time, I will be a bringer, then not.'

'We, walkers, are gendered from birth. We ... I.' Ash stopped speaking, but its neume was a tangle of feelings and images.

'I feel it.' Rong focused inward allowing Ash's thoughts permeate into ter understanding. 'Your body is seed, but your spirit is egg. I feel the pain of this conflict in you.' *Comfort*, Rong neumed in return. 'This is your ... wrongness. Walkers don't accept this state of being?'

'Some people see it as wrong and strange. Some don't. It can be hard.'

Rong received thought images of Ash's challenges—*aloneness*. 'Your pod is fearful of your *gender* nature. My pod fears my legs.'

'Yeah, my pod ... my family want me to stop changing to female ... egg bringer.'

'It is just change. Abrax change. At each proliferation we bring egg or seed.'

'Wow. You change gender, and that's normal. Maybe your pod would accept me.'

'No. You have legs.'

Ash grabbed Rong's hands. I accept your legs. I accept how you are. The way you are saved me. You are not wrong. You need a better name.' Ash held tight. Images flooded into Rong's mind. *Strong trees near shining water - birds screeching-swooping-diving to hunt fish.* After a long cool moment together in the darkness, Ash whispered. 'Marsh.'

'Marsh,' the Abrax repeated. 'This place, where land and water are together.'

'Yes. In the marshes, the wetlands, life is strong and unique and everything mixes together. You are strong and unique. You belong in both the water and on the land. Marsh is a perfect name.'

10

In His Image

'What if I just moved the shoulders down a bit? Maybe to T5? You know, a bit more of a starfish effect?'

'What's wrong with the blueprint we've got?'

'I'm just sick of making the same old thing day after day. I thought it would be a nice change, to mix it up a bit. You know, I think they'd look good with ... five even appendages radiating from a central body ... starfish style, but walking, and still with a face ... just to change it up a bit.'

'And how would you explain it to Him? He'd probably have you sent back to worm assembly.

Your eyesight isn't so good anymore, so you'd be slower. Less units produced means less pay.'

'But there's so much scope here in homo-sapiens ... it makes me feel so creative.'

'Shhh. Watch what you're saying. You know He's the only one who can call himself a creator - *the* creator.'

'I know, but just have a look what I've done with it before I fix it up for dispatch.'

'It certainly looks starfish-esque. That neck would take some getting used to, and I can't see how the shorter legs will be an advantage.'

'But the overall height is unaffected.'

'Okay, so now you've gotten the *creativity* out of your system, I'll help you rearrange the components. This would never get through quality control.'

'I've slipped things through before ... remember the chicken and the egg anomaly?'

'Was that you?'

'Yep, and look how well that turned out.'

'But this time, there'll be no egg to hide things in.'

'Oh, they'll just blame it on science ... evolution ... mutation. They've stopped blaming things like this on us, now that they have science.'

'But what about Him? He might turn a blind eye to the other departments when there's a slip-up, but he takes this department, *His* department very seriously.'

'Yeah – yeah. I know the motto, *in His image*.'

'It's what He wants.'

'But that's not what we do. Look at all the variations ... male, female, black, yellow, pink ... hairy, bald, tall, short, fat thin, dumb, smart. So what image is He after? I mean, what was He doing with those prototypes?'

'You mean the hairy ones with the long arms and the big foreheads?'

'Yeah. He didn't keep them as *His image* for long.'

'It's not our job to question. We just follow the blueprints and assemble.'

'Maybe He'll like my alterations?'

'Send that thing through to quality control and you'll be back assembling worms before you know it.'

11

Two Glasses

Lara's voice was watery, trickling away to become another echo soaking into the thick stone walls of the old cottage. She sat alone picking a favourite melody on her guitar. It too sounded diluted, without the throaty rhythms of Phillip's guitar that had accompanied her until two weeks ago.

Then Phillip's harmony was in the room, faint and momentary, perhaps the stone walls had soaked up the echoes he had once played and were now releasing them. A draft tickled across her shoulders. Her song caught in her throat, she gripped the neck of her guitar to deaden the strings and walked over, leaning it against the brick chimney.

Her hand brushed the stone on the other side of the hearth where Phillip's guitar used to rest. The empty space felt chilled. There were many empty spaces now that he had taken his stuff and left the cottage — their cottage.

Memories swirled through Lara's mind. Nearly two years ago they'd moved into this timeworn four and a half room cottage. The front half of the house was the original stone, more than a century old, a sitting room and a bedroom. Up a twist of narrow stairs was an attic room with a steeply pitched roof, a tiny window and dark wooden shelves lining one wall. They used this weird nook for reading. In the back of the house, under a low slanting ceiling, were two rooms that served as poor approximations of kitchen and bathroom, with a laundry-hallway combo separating them which also opened into a small backyard.

The rental agent had described these added rooms as retro gems from the 1950s. The cottage had felt cosy and romantic. Now Lara was on her own and it felt different, peculiar. Things creaked and rattled. There were echoes of tunes and words. She knew it had to be the stress of the heartache, Phillip leaving. She wasn't sleeping well, so, of course she was feeling a little unhinged, spooked. She knew she should be kinder to herself, but the weird sensations over the past two weeks were getting to her and getting more frequent.

It was hard enough getting used to Phillip's mysterious exit from her life, without wondering if she was losing her grip on reality. She'd been misplacing things and going to do things that she had already done, not remembering having done them. The echoes in the half-empty house seemed to be morphing into real sounds, foot-steps and faint music that quietened before she could be sure she'd heard it. Fragrances that wafted through the house then faded. It all seemed so real.

Lara wasn't inclined to say things like spirits or ghosts, not out loud. She had gone to visit a tarot reader a few weeks ago. Nellie from work said she was a regular visitor to a place called

Eclectic Esoteric, which was some kind of crystal shop, and she had invited her to come and have a tarot card reading one day. Lara had been curious, so she'd gone. The tiny shop had an amazing vibe. It was crammed with shelves full of books and tarot decks wrapped in yellowing cellophane. Crystals and jewellery filled every gap on the narrow shelves. The card reader – Constance – had surprised her by saying things that Lara had not told anyone about and she made some predictions that Lara pushed to the back of her mind until weeks after the reading when those wisps of insight became truths.

Lara once studied some psychology at university, she knew of theories about how humans unconsciously share images and symbols. She believed in happenstance, serendipity. Just like when she and Phillip found the advertisement for the cottage by accident. Some of their friends said the place was creepy, but they felt content living here. The cottage didn't feel the same any more. 'It's nothing ... stress ... the break-up.' Lara words echoed. 'He gave no warning ... no reason ... just two text messages.'

Her words dissolved into sobbing. The desperate, sad noise bounced inside the empty spaces, the chorus of her despair whirled around her and there was something else, another sound, faint deep vibrating. Again she could hear Phillip's guitar, and the deep cadent tones that had always tangled around her melody. Her sobbing stopped and she held her breath. The guitar was really there — wasn't it? Then it faded. 'Musical hallucinations, that's all I need.' She took a deep breath, the air smelt spicy. She sniffled and reached for a tissue, blowing her nose unmusically. Stretching her tense neck muscles, she threw the crumpled tissues away and walked towards the twisting stairs, heading up to the reading nook, determined to distract herself.

Weak afternoon light spilled through the dormered window. On each side of the window were lumpy armchairs she and Phillip had found sitting on the side of the road just after they'd moved in. The books sat on the shelves like crooked teeth, leaning over where they fell in to the gaps left when Phillip took his. A small pile of dog-eared novels he'd missed sat on his chair. She reached and touched a cover gently. Her breathed hitched. 'I suppose these are mine now.' She swallowed a sob. 'You can never have too many books.' She picked up her own book from her chair and sat, purposefully turning her back on the other chair and the forgotten pile. Her tired eyes fought to keep the words from blurring into a grey mess as she read.

Lara woke suddenly. The house creaked and shuddered in the darkness. The air felt icy in the attic room, she reached up and pulled her rug from the high back of her chair, shrugged it around her shoulders and groped for the switch on the table lamp. Her heart flipped. Phillip's books were gone from the chair.

'He's here.' She stood and wobbled then remembered that he'd left the keys and she had added an extra lock to ease her nerves about living alone. She tightened her grip on the rug and crept downstairs to check the locks. The front door was rarely used and was locked. Windows where all locked. Back door was also locked. She flicked on the kitchen light. Phillip's books were piled into the bin next to the stove. 'First it's musical hallucinations and now I'm sleep-cleaning ... I'm so losing the plot.' The feeble joke didn't make her feel better. She put the books on the table, and grabbed the wine from the fridge.

The wine had helped Lara sleep for some of the night, but her sleep had been broken by noises and she'd lay waiting and listening in the dark. Her day at work dragged on, but after a comforting dinner of pasta from the local take-out, Lara felt content and headed up to the nook to read.

Something felt different as she climbed up into the darkness. The tiny room felt icy and buzzed with static. Reaching out, feeling for the switch on the lamp, the hairs on her arms prickled. As golden light from the lamp filled the room, there was a flicker out of the corner of her vision. She looked towards the book shelf and her face flushed with heat. The books. Yesterday they were gap-toothed reminders of Phillip's departure. This evening they had been straightened. Alphabetised. Book-ends shuffled up into place. She stepped slowly over and reach out her hand, her fingers crackled as she touched the books. She had drunk a little too much wine last night, but she didn't remember sorting them. 'I must have done it.' She shook her head and shivered, a chilly current of air swirled over her skin. Reaching for her rug, she pulled it around her shoulders and sat, hugging her unopened book and staring at the bookshelf. Something moaned out in the darkness. She jumped and dropped her book, her heart thumping up into her throat. 'Get a grip, Lara.' She took a slow breath and retrieved the book. 'It's just Horny Cat starting up his nightly serenade.'

In the warn pool of lamp-light, Lara read and re-read the same page. The words made less sense each time, so she headed down stairs. On a whim, she picked up her guitar and slumped down onto the sofa to noodle around with some melodies. 'I played before Phillip and I love guitar too much, so now, I'm a soloist.' The guitar was a warm curve, pressed against her ribs. She felt the narrow stiffness of the strings pressing into her finger-tips as she found notes on the neck. Her right hand fell into familiar patterns, picking the strings and the music resonated deep in her chest. Her heart fell into rhythm with the music and Lara was just playing. No thinking, no worrying.

There was music, faint, far-away. Lara fumbled hitting sour notes. She stopped, listened — nothing. She picked up at the next phrase and played on. There it was again. She shook her head and bent down over the guitar's neck, determined to ignore her over-active imagination.

The musical chimera rose to a crescendo. Lara played louder to drown it out. A massive minor chord change resonated around the room. Lara froze and listened, but the accompaniment was already fading, just an echo. 'No. I'm not losing it, or being haunted, which equals losing it.' Lara stood and leaned her guitar against the chimney. 'It's just my amazing musical memory.' There was a yowl in the darkness. 'Shit. That horny cat—' She walked to the kitchen, flicked on the light and grabbed a tattered tennis ball off the bench. She opened the back door and lobbed the ball at the fence. The cat hissed as the ball thumped the wood. Lara slammed the door shut and headed in to run a bath. Soon the air was filled with the scent of frankincense and neroli.

At work the next day, Lara was nowhere near as rested as she had been after wine night. Her sleep had been full of echoing melodies and low-voiced harmonies. She had tossed and turned, waking often and straining to listen into the darkness.

'How's it going?' asked Nellie as Lara reached for coffee before heading to her desk.

Lara didn't look up. 'Good.' She lifted the cup and inhaled the aroma deeply.

'You look a bit shit.' Nellie rubbed Lara's shoulder.

'I'm not sleeping well.'

'I thought you were getting used to the creaks and groans of Grandma's cottage.'

'Ha – ha, Nellie.' Lara sipped her coffee. 'I thought I was getting used to it too, but … the noises are just—'

'Just what, Lara?'

'I'm feeling a bit … unhinged. The noises sometimes sound like … music. Words. And things are moved, tidied up and I don't remember doing it.'

'So you have a ghost-maid. Cool.'

'Shut up, Nellie. It's—' A tear ran down Lara's cheek and plopped into her coffee.

'Hey. Sorry.' Nellie put Lara's cup on the bench and hugged her. 'I know this has been tough. I know you've hardly slept since Phillip left. No wonder you're forgetting you did things.' She handed back the coffee. 'Drink up. You'll get better at sleeping alone. Just give it time.'

'When I try to sleep my mind churns, then it's full of dreams.' Lara shook her head and sipped.

'I get like that sometimes. When I do, I go to *Eclectic Esoteric*, get my cards read, get some advice, maybe a crystal.' Nellie reached for the coffee. 'We could go, like before. I'll ring and make an appointment with Constance.'

'Thank you,' said Lara. 'Constance was lovely, and it was fun, but I don't know if ... I don't want this to be all ghosty and woo-woo. I just want sleep.'

'Woo-woo?' Nellie laughed.

'I'm sorry. Constance was really good. Some of the stuff she saw in my cards last time even sort of happened ... I don't know what I'm saying.'

'It's all good.' Nellie squeezed Lara's shoulder. 'Let me know if you decide to seek out the woo-woo.' She laughed. 'In the meantime, Zumba, followed by tapas and wine. My treat. That'll help you sleep.'

Zumba and wine had helped Lara sleep. She dozed through three reminders on her snooze alarm and raced through a shower. When she entered the 50s kitchen to grab a quick breakfast, the books were back in the bin and a loan carnation was sitting in a coffee mug in the centre of the table. Lara felt suddenly dizzy and started backing out of the kitchen. She grabbed the door jamb and took a breath. 'It must have been Nellie.' She had probably done this after she'd delivered Lara to bed after Zumba and tapas and wine.

After her most restful night since Phillip had left, work made sense and Lara had accepted an invite from Ruth at reception and some concerned work mates to go out for lunch. 'I hope we've helped bring her back from the dark side,' Ruth laughed as they piled the left over Chinese food into take-out tubs.

Lara allowed herself a moment to think about the dark side, all the strangeness at night-times. She shuddered and shrugged it off. That was behind her now she had slept well last night. Things were getting back to a new normal. The afternoon in the office was easy, fun. The bus had arrived on time and wasn't even crowded.

'No excuses, today,' Lara said to herself and the horny cat, who sat on the path licking himself. He stopped licking and gazed up at as she unlocked the back door. She shoved the left-overs from lunchtime into the fridge, threw her bag on the sofa and went straight into her bedroom. In minutes she had changed into her running gear and was back outside, jogging up the driveway past Horny, who had resumed his licking.

As the sun was setting, Lara returned home sweaty but relaxed. Horny started yowling from his usual night-time spot on the fence. She picked up a tennis ball and went back outside. 'Shut up, Horny,' she warned. 'No one cares about your failed love life.' She lobbed the ball into the shadows. The fence palings rattled, Horny yelped and took off down the side path.

When Lara stepped back inside, she could hear the bath running. Steamy air, scented with frankincense and neroli drifted out into the afterthought hallway-laundry. Did she start running the bath? She really wanted a bath, she must have. Despite the warm steam, her skin prickled with cool static as she walked into the bathroom. Everything was as she always arranged things for a bath. She shrugged off the shiver, then checked all the rooms and the locks while the bath filled.

After her bath Lara felt more normal and relaxed than she had done for days, and hungry. 'Two options.' Her stomach rumbled. 'Vegemite toast or the left over Chinese from lunch.' She grabbed the left overs out of the fridge. This rented 50's kitchen didn't have a microwave oven. She took a pot from the cupboard, slid the cold blob of left-overs out of the tub and moved to place the pot on the stove. The hot plate was already on. A prickly static licked at Lara's arm as she dropped the pot on the heat. She pulled away, the tingled flowed through her shoulder and into her chest. 'Wine.' The word was shrill. 'Wine.' She went to the sideboard that held the glasses and the wine rack. Put the wine and glasses on the table. Turned to check the warming left-overs. Guitar music rippled. She took a deep breath. 'Wine.' Turned back towards the table. 'Oh shit! Two glasses ... like we always did ... before.' Tears blurred the wine bottle, but she couldn't un-see the two glasses. Her mind swirling with memories of the hundreds of other times there had been two glasses sitting there and that had been a wonderful thing. Now the second glass taunted her. She walked over blew her nose, loud and gross, straightened her shoulders and turned to put the other glass away. Cool air swirled, tickling her shoulder. The stove timer rang, even though she didn't remember setting it. She turned. One of the glasses was hovering in mid-air, half way between the table and the sideboard. Then it dropped—smashed on the green and pink retro tiles.

Lara froze. The timer bell rattled. She thumped it off. Guitar music echoed in from the lounge room. She gulped in jagged breaths as she rummaged in her bag for her phone. 'Can you book for me to see Constance?' she blurted before Nellie had a chance to say hello.

Eclectic Esoteric was only three times as wide as its door. An elaborately styled sign with gold lettering swayed gently, held in the claws of a wrought iron dragon that loomed out over the sidewalk above the entrance. Wind-chimes tied to the back of the door tinkled as Lara stepped inside. The air was thick with incense and energy. Lara drew a deep breath. As she exhaled, she let her shoulders relax. It had been a long night. After she'd cleaned up the glass, she hadn't slept much waiting for the next weird thing to happen.

The narrow shop was a cluttered rainbow of boxes, books, prayer flags, wall hangings, and crystals. In every gap, clusters of jagged colour, strings of polished beads, smooth crystal orbs resting in nests of driftwood. Light danced between the shining surfaces like sunshine on water. 'I'm here for a ... reading.' Lara said as she steadied herself against the counter.

'Welcome back, Lara.' Constance pushed through a curtain at the back of the shop. 'Nellie called and said she'd given you her time.' Constance shimmered and rattled as she walked. 'She said something about a woo-woo emergency.' Her lavender eyebrows raised and she smiled. Then she squeezed her thin strong arm around Lara's shoulders and steered her into the small shadowy room behind the curtain. The room was warm and its edges were softened with shadows and pools of warm light.

They sat at a small table draped with deep blue velvet, while Constance shuffled her worn tarot cards. 'So...' Her hands gentle and unrushed as the cards flitted past each other. 'Nellie says you're, "troubled", not sleeping since your man left you.'

'Sounds like a country song.' Lara forced a weak laugh.

'Hold the cards.' She handed the tattered deck to Lara. 'Let them know what you think would help you.'

Lara's held the cards tightly. Her mind swirled with all the strangeness and heart ache of the past few weeks. The fear, of what, being haunted or being insane? Her breath shuddered. Constance took Lara's hands in hers and stared. She smiled and her dark eyes sparkled. 'You are stronger and more astounding than you realise.'

She slipped the cards from Lara's hands and arranged them on the velvet. Touching each in turn, nodding, smiling, pausing, staring as though a cards were windows. 'He's like a wandering knight. The one who left you, he's gone seeking.' She shrugged. 'His quest was his alone.' *That explained as little as the two text messages Phillip sent.*

'I do see a male, someone else close by, not romance but a strong affection, a desire for your attention. Singing? Beseeching?'

'The cat!' Lara laughed. 'He's on the fence every night, yowling. He drives me crazy.'

'Pat him. That's all he wants.'

Constance touched each card and spoke generally of success at work and how strong Lara's links to her women friends were. Small reassurances about family members. 'Your home ... has been a sanctuary for you, but lately things have become unsettled.'

'It's an old house, always creaking and rattling.' Lara justified. 'Maybe I never noticed the noises when there was two of us.' Her breath jagged as she spoke. 'But now there's voices, music, things are moving, or maybe I'm nuts.'

'Many believe there is more to us than simply our physical nature.' Constance tapped her polished lavender nails on a card, the wheel of fortune. 'We can turn our dreams into reality if we desire them enough. Desires and thoughts are dynamic electrical impulses, energy, and they are as real as we believe them to be. These thoughts connect us to our past and conjure our future.' Constance turned and took a small box from the shelf behind her, placing it on the table. 'Sometimes all these thoughts and desires can tangle up our spirit.' She opened the box and lifted out a silver frame the shape of a triangular pyramid. A crystal star hung inside the apex.

'It's very pretty.' The sparkling grey star reflected the soft light in the room. Lara counted eight triangular facets, the top most one was cradled in a silver clasp attached to the pyramid.

'It's a merkaba. A star tetrahedron.' Constance tapped one of the points and it spun, light bounced of each facet. 'Light, spirit and body. All connected. The merkaba will help you untangle your spirit and your worries. They will be drawn into the smoky quartz. It will help you deal with your troubles.'

'I just want to get some sleep.'

'Wear it during the day.' Constance unhooked the merkaba from its cradle and slid the silver loop onto a chain. 'And sleep with it next to your bed. Your thoughts will be drawn into the crystal until you see how to resolve things for yourself.'

Constance leaned across the table and placed the long chain over Lara's head. The crystal felt warm against her skin. Her heart fluttered and slowed.

That night Lara placed the merkaba in its cradle and set it on the table next to her bed. Sleep was deep but different, brimming with dreams. In the dreams she was inside the hazy version of her cottage, wandering through all the days since Phillip's departure. She could see the sad Lara pacing and tearful or singing alone, watched her drinking alone. Next, she saw her huddled in her chair in the reading nook, jumping at every noise.

As the dream continued and deepened, Lara was enjoying the return of the feeling of calm she had always felt in the little cottage. In these vivid dreams, she had no doubt that this calm of the dreams would return with time. She wished she could let the sad, misty Lara know things would get better. Yes, she would make things better.

All at once, Lara was back to the afternoon weeks ago in the reading nook. She watched her sad-self touch Phillip's books then turn her back on them. Lara felt anger for the cowardly way Phillip left with no explanation. She stepped past herself, now sleeping in the chair, and snatched up Phillip's piled books and turned, instantly she was in the kitchen, she dropped the pile of books in the bin. Her heart felt light.

Horny Cat yowled. She smiled, deciding to sing him a song, she took her guitar, sat on the sofa, and played. The cat yowled on, suddenly she was at the fence with him and scratching him under the chin. He quieted and purred.

Turning from the cat, she was back in the reading nook, looking at the gap-toothed book self. She shuffled and reordered the books until the gaps were gone. Turning again, she was in the kitchen. Sad Lara was there too and the cat yowled and she watched as a tennis ball was thrown into the darkness.

Next, she was sitting on the edge of the bath, surrounded by swirling clouds of steam. Now there was crying from the kitchen and she was there watching herself staring at the two glasses.

As she went to move the glass, she could see the facets sparkled through her translucent flesh and suddenly the glass was heavy. So heavy. It fell through her flimsy hand and smashed of the pink and green floor.

Lara jarred awake. In the darkness the merkaba twirled catching glints of moonlight — and she knew who her ghost had been.

12

Walls

Tana plunged her hand into the bucket of cold mud, churning the straw and ooze into a thick daub. The walls always leaked when the rain came in strong, blowing sideways on the wind, washing the daub out of the eye sockets. The empty eyes would stream muddy tears, signalling time for repairs.

If Tana didn't seal up the leaky eyes, then the tears would stream down the bone cheeks, dripping down from skull to skull until the walls became unstable. A skull or two would tumble out laying sideways, staring up with half-faced smiles.

When Tana was very tired, she almost heard the half-smiles teasing her.

We can be seen again. All the sadness will come out of peoples' hearts because you let us and the memories out of the mud.

Cover us up quick, before they see us weeping.

So many hours, packing the skulls and the past behind the mud. As if any one would ever forget our walls were made of skulls and why that was so. Why hide their bravery away when they could be celebrated? Tana shivered as the cold of the daub crept up her arm. Keeper of the Memories sounded like an honourable position to hold in the community, but all it meant was that she didn't weep and swoon when her name was drawn out for the job. Keeper really meant 'keep the skulls covered' so that folk could walk around town and ignore that the only thing left to build with was the bones of the brave.

Now those brave faces had to wear a mask of mud to save the sensibilities of less brave folk. Tana slapped an angry handful of daub onto a teary skull. Seized by her own disrespect, she paused and smoothed the mud down and around the dark-curve. Her hand brushed a leaf. Small, shiny. She flicked at it, but it held its place. Rubbing it between a muddy finger and thumb, she realised the tiny leaf was a seed that had taken root in the shelter of an eye socket. This first greenness of early spring filled Tana with defiant inspiration.

For the next week, Tana carefully selected new and secret aggregates to blend the daub. After days of rain, many dead eyes were now open. She remained busy mixing and mending throughout the lengthening spring days.

A smiling woman came out of the cottage where Tana was daubing and gave her some juice and a dumpling. 'Keeper, thank you. My heart is lifted by your commitment to the Memories.'

My compliance in hiding our past. Tana ate her snack and returned to her work. Everyone's house had the bones of someone they loved or respected holding up the roof. Those people had sacrificed to keep others safe and even now they still kept them safe. The brave deserved more than to be muddied and ignored. Tana hoped folk would see it her way.

Spring rains gave way to the baking heat of summer. Now Tana's work was to moisten the walls so that they didn't crack and make small repairs when they did. The mud was warmer now and Tana was keen to keep a careful watch on her walls.

In the quiet of a too warm afternoon, the call rang out through the drowsing community. 'The eyes of the brave are full of blossoms.'

Tana was quick to start a wave of positive thought. 'It's a miracle,' she said into many an ear as she moved closer to the commotion. Her words were echoed as folk gathered.

'It's a miracle.'

'A miraculous wonder.'

'Keeper, what do you make of this?'

Tana looked around with rehearsed surprise. Then stared with distant meditative contemplation and spoke quietly. 'The spirit of our brave protectors is strong. The fragrant blossoms are here to ease our hearts and provide for our needs.'

With wondrous good timing, a child walked forward and sniffed at the tiny flowers and smiled.

'And the roots spreading through the walls will strengthen them, holding our families safe and sound against the elements.' She held her breath and waited to see if her secret work would fail.

In twos and threes, folk drew closer to the wall. Reaching brave fingers to touch the plants budding from the skulls. Then they turned toward their own homes to look for blossoms.

At the end of that summer, Tana's position was renamed, Keeper of the Spirit Gardens. She no longer struggled alone maintaining the walls. Now a team of keepers harvested herbs and foods. They gathered seeds and planned for new seasons' planting. Tana still mixed the daub to create a fitting commemoration for the brave ones who had wished and sacrificed for a better future.

13

I was Frances

'Well, my beautiful nameless girl, we're all waiting to see when you'll decide to sleep.' Rhoda gazed down at her new granddaughter as she wriggled and stared around. 'You have a long life ahead of you to see the world. You should close your eyes a while.' The baby squirmed as Rhoda kissed her.

'Nup.' The baby muttered and wriggled some more.

'Nup, hey.' Rhoda smiled and started pacing, rocking the restless babe. 'Your mummy and daddy are snuggled in bed. You've worn them out.

They're too tired to even decide on a name for you.'

Rhoda padded quietly to the kitchen in case the baby made a fuss and woke her parents. 'Grandma had a long nap today, so I'm on night duty. Come on precious girl, close those eyes.' Rhoda cooed as she rocked the wide-eyed baby. 'You'll have your mum and dad frantic if they wake up in the morning and see that you still haven't gone to sleep.'

'Nup sleep.' The baby muttered and looked straight into Rhoda's eyes and smiled. Rhoda wobbled and sat on the cushion of the window seat.

'Maybe I didn't get as much sleep as I thought.' Rhoda stared at the wriggling baby. She was turning her head, looking around the kitchen then looked back to Rhoda.

'Nup baby.'

'What?' Rhoda shook her head, looking around to see that she was alone.

'Not baby,' the tiny voice mumbled.

Rhoda stared. Her heart pounding. Her mouth opened, but what could she say. She was having a chat with her very young grand-daughter. 'I must look this up on line. I must have some kind of proud grand-parent syndrome.' She laughed at herself. 'I'm chatting with you.' She cooed at the baby. 'And you aren't talking back because you're just a baby.'

'Not—a—baby.' The words, though still quiet, were clearer now. The little eyes brimmed with tears.

Rhoda reacted from instinct, gently wiping away the tiny tears. 'Oh sweetie.' Rhoda cooed. 'What's making you so sad.'

'I—miss—Henry.'

'Wow.' Rhoda felt suddenly hot. She leaned against the cool window pane and let out a shaky breath. 'They're real words.' Flabbergasted, she swallowed, smiled down at the little face and asked, 'Who is Henry?'

'My husband. My love. He was holding my hand. And now—' The small awkward words melted into tears.

Rhoda's heart thumped. Words like ghost and possession swam around inside her head, out of all the words that spun, her unlikely and unspoken choice was reincarnation. Whatever was happening, this tiny, sad person was feeling alone and needed comfort.

'What's your name?'

'Frances Andrews. I was Frances. But now—'

Rhoda knew all about feeling frightened and alone. She breathed deeply and, wiping more tears from the tiny cheeks then said, 'Tell me about Henry.' She watched and listened as her tiny precious grand-daughter spoke about another life time.

'It feels like we've loved each other for ever.' The baby stared into a place full of memories that only she could see. 'We were married so young, in the spring of fifty-eight.' The little smile broadened. 'Sixty-four years ... we went down the coast on our honeymoon. I sat behind him on his motorcycle, hugged him for hours. No helmets back then, Henry gave me a scarf to cover my hair.'

'It sounds like you had an adventurous life.' Rhoda stroked the baby cheek and her little eyes drooped, then flashed open.

'I don't want to sleep. I want to remember.' Frances wriggled in Rhoda's arms. 'We built a house together, in Barrington. Lived there all our lives. It was just me and him, no kids came our way, so yes we had lots of adventures. We travelled all over. Climbing, boating, caving, skiing.' She laughed softly. 'He said the biggest challenge was when I insisted we learn Latin dancing.' The laughter filled with tears. 'But this was the biggest challenge for him ... holding my hand as I left him alone.'

'Henry has all those memories too. He has you forever in his heart.' Rhoda knew that memories don't fill all the gaps. She hugged Frances close.

'I was frightened. Henry rubbed his hand so gently across my forehead, just like he always did when I was upset. He held my hand all through the night. The last thing I saw was his loving eyes gazing at me. Who will hold his hand?'

'Would you like me to check on Henry? Barrington's not far. I'm sure he'd like to know about this amazing adventure.'

'Yes ... that's kind of you.'

'I would be my honour, he's sort of family now.' Rhoda smiled, but her tears flowed.

'I know it's time to go around again,' said Frances. 'But the memories are too wonderful to let go.'

'Tell me some more,' said Rhoda.

'He taught me to ride his motorcycle—I crashed it—in the creek—he laughed—mud fight.' Frances laughed. The laughed faded into gurgling, then sighing. Her eyelids drooped slowly.

'It's good to know you, Frances. Welcome to our family. We love you very much.'

'Frances?' The sleepy voice of Rhoda's daughter came from the kitchen doorway.

'Yes, the baby and I had a long talk during the night.' Rhoda ran her thumb gently across the last fading worry line on the new-old brow and smiled. 'She told me to call her Frances.'

'That's a pretty name,' said her son-in-law.

'A little old fashioned, but lovely for when she's older,' said her daughter.

Rhoda stared at the baby's sleeping face. The old woman's story was over now. It was time for her grand-daughter's story to start. 'Yes, Frances, but let's call her Frankie for now.'

14

Swan Song

Power can conjure a false sense of privilege. The belief that you are more-than, which leads to the notion that others are less-than. If that power is magical, then that sense of privilege might have no constraints.

Magnus was such a magical man. This warlock, was true to the old meaning of the word. He was a traitor to his kind, using his power to any and all ends that met his predilections. And for the moment that was an all-consuming penchant for birds. He was a lover of birds, in particular, swans, and would stand at the river bank for hours, staring at his favourite swan. The graceful curve of her sinuous neck. The fulsome roundness of her smooth breast. The flowing skirt of silken plumage as she waltzed and weaved through the river currents and glided under the dappled willow shadows at the water's edge.

Magnus imagined the transformation of this magnificent, alluring creature into his very own swan-woman. He imagined himself dancing with her. Holding her in his arms. Kissing her shiny, red transformed lips. She, staring lovingly at him, her ebony eyes glistening. He would enchant her, weaving her will to his own. Then he would caress those smooth breasts and ruffle those flowing skirts, and he would truly be a bird-lover. He laughed at his own cleverness.

As the moon waxed he pondered and prepared gathering the freshest, sweetest corn and delicate spinach leaves, and working his magic on them. On the evening of the full moon, he strode off to the river's edge. Magnus wrapped himself in a magical glimmer that transformed him into a majestic swan, gleaming white with a neck band of speckled sable. With the corn and spinach perch on his back he glided into the river's flow.

Her name was Sena. They glided together in the moonlight, and by-and-by, she accepted his gifts of food and his offer to be her mate. Magnus could see the potion in the food he offered was working. First her eyes became brighter and wider as she stared into his. Then her skirts of feathers started to ruffle and loosen, floating away on the rippling current. Magnus swept her up into his wings and glided them both towards the river's edge. The last of her feathers fell away, and he lay his naked swan-woman on the mossy bank. That night he was truly a bird-lover, until the rising sun unworked his magic.

Magnus could and did, return to the river and his ensorcelled lover whenever the urge took him. Swans take one partner for life, but Magnus soon tired of his swooning swan-bride. He and his proclivities pursued other alluring and exploitable species.

Sena fretted for her missing mate. The five eggs in her nest twitched under her warm feather skirt.

These signets needed their father. Why had he not returned? She tucked her beak in under her feathers and sleep fitfully, dreaming strange dreams of dancing with human legs and cold chills of mud on bare, featherless skin.

Inside the eggs, the hatchlings grew restless, ready to be in the world. Small cracks appeared. It was time. The signets struggled to be free from the eggs. In Sena's reckoning, it was a long unnatural struggle. The eggs rolled and her babies thrashed, squalling inside. She wept in her heart and began to peck away the shell.

Wet matted feathers glistened, black feet pushed, wriggled, pushed. As Sena's first little one twisted free from its shell, she saw the sable marking of her mate on the youngling's neck. She stilled herself, ready to meet its shiny black eyes and bond at first sight as her kind always did.

The black eyes twisted free of the shell and Sena reared back in fear and shock. The tiny damp signet stared up at her with a human face. It squalled and flopped out of its egg. Instinct took hold, and Sena pushed the squalling hatchling into the warmth under her feather skirt. This vision of the strange bird must have come from the grief over losing her mate. She turned to help free the other clutchlings from their eggs and each in-turn squalled at her with a human face. She pushed each quickly under her feathers. Tucking her own head under her wing, she shook with fear and grief. Weeping her way into troubled sleep, she dreamt again of cold mud on bare skin. Her sable necked mate melting like spring snow until he too had a human face.

She woke in the pale dawn hearing strange mumblings from under her feather skirts. Her hatchlings' chittering was mixed with curious sounds. Murmuring both familiar and far off—words. Her signets chittered and chirped, and talked. She recognised the sounds of human talk, but now she also understood it's meaning. How could she or her brood know human words?

'Of course you know the words,' said her first hatched, pushing out between the feathers. 'You have been human.'

Sena twisted her curved neck up proudly. 'I am a swan. How could I be anything else?'

'Think of your sable necked mate. Think hard and remember.'

'How can you know of your father?'

'Because he is our father ... which gives us his magic.' Each of her younglings took turns to explain the magician deceptions and violation. With each detail shared, Sena's disbelief grew to heart-break. She truly loved her mate and swan nature made the love last a life-time, but for her human faced brood things were different. They knew their mother faced an impossible task, caring for them all without her mate beside her. They watched as Sena slumped in the reeds, inconsolable, and their young hearts festered with loathing. The hatchlings huddled together. Speaking in human whispers, they planned their magical revenge.

The signets busied themselves in preparation, gathering plants and magical agents from here and there along the river bank. At sun set, they snuggled and preened with their mother. When the moon rose, they clambered up onto her back. 'Please take us up into the brook, dear Mother.'

Sena paddled hard against the current throughout the night. As the pale light of day crept into the sky, the chittered. 'Here, Mother. Here. Bring us to shore.'

On the bank, stood a small, well-appointed cottage. Neatly mortared stone walls, windows paned with real glass. A low fence of woven brambles surrounded a cornucopian garden, lush with fruit trees, vegetables and herbs.

'What is this place?' Sena asked.

'Our father's house,' the signets muttered as they busied themselves off loading their magical cargo.

A thin trail of smoke from the chimney showed someone was at home, but the house was in darkness. Sena quivered with fear and concealed herself in the reads at the water edge and watched as her unnatural brood toddled towards the cottage.

Inside, all was dark, but with magical eyes the signets could see. At the back of the cottage Magnus slept the deep sated sleep of a lover. His arm draped across the half transformed body. His conquest lay with bare legs twitching and shining in the low pre-dawn light. The magic was unmaking itself. The legs melted into smooth grey at the thighs. The arms were shrinking and flattening as the signets watched. The chest and shoulders moved and melted like grey snow as the doomed lover's hair fell away and her sleeping face swelled on the pillow until she was once more a porpoise.

The signets could only stare and hold their rage in check. Their work was all the more vindicated now. As the last vestiges of pale legs fused back into a fleshy tail, the hatchlings, clambered onto the table and poured their potion into the magician's wine. Then they pattered into the larder and sprinkled his greens and corn with magical herbs.

The first rays of sunlight came through the window reaching across to the bed. As they fell on the sleeping porpoise morphling, she roused. Screeching with panicked confusion, she flicked out her tail defensively, flinging herself onto the cobbled floor. As she thrashed, her smooth skin scraped on the stone.

Magnus woke startled. He held down the thrashing creature then poured a vial of something into her mouth and she stilled. He wrapped her in a cloth. The signets saw the creature's blood soaking through. Magnus dragged his porpoise lover down to the river's edge and rolled her out of the cloth and into the swallows. She twitched and roused, twisting and thrashing her tail until she disappeared into the river's flow.

The magician returned to the cottage. The signets hid themselves in the shrinking shadows. Magnus flung the bloody sheet in the fire and slumped onto a chair. He poured himself some wine from the carafe on the table, sipping as he watched the cloth smoulder on the hearth. He refilled his glass and the hatchlings smiled their strange smiles at each other. They watched, gleeful, as Magnus rummaged in his larder, taking the food they had seasoned with magical herbs. He ate and drank in a frenzy as the hatchlings had intended in their magic. The morning brightened outside, but Magnus blinked his shiny black eyes drowsily. He waddled over to his bed and slept.

The signets found their mother hiding in the reeds, and were thankful she had not seen their father's evil actions. They clambered up onto their mother again and answered all her questions as best they dared as the current returned them to the bend in the river that is their home.

The hatchlings, for all their strange magic, needed to snuggle into Sena's feather skirts and sleep the day away. At sunset they tottered about the riverbank as Sena busied herself trying to gather enough food for the hungry brood. As the sun turned red and dropped low in the sky, Sena saw a swan paddling around the river's bend. A handsome swan with a sable band at its neck.

The brood watched from the nest, cautious for any signs of magic or memory in their transformed father, but there were none. They saw in their magical hearts that he remembered only that he is Sena's life mate. Magnus nudged Sena back to her nest and as the light faded, he foraged for food and brought it to the magical signets that peaked their strange faces out from under Sena's feather skirts.

One day in late summer, it was time for the brood to go from their mother. As the sun set, the brood paddled into the shadows, singing and humming their special magic to ease their mother's grief at their leaving. As the magical music faded, so did the last of Sena's summer memories. The swan couple come together, necks twining, to spin and dance on the river's gentle current. Dreaming of next summer and all the other summer and signets they will raise together.

It is said that on warm nights, at this particular bend in the river, you can hear mysterious melodies and, on these nights, the swans glide and spin together on the water until the moon is high.

15

Pay it Backwards

It was frightening to see the tiny child disappear as the wave crashed down, swallowing her into the churning green-blue. It was horrifying for Netta to remember what it felt like to be pummeled against the sand and not knowing which way was up, being twisted and beaten by the force of that wave. She watched, shaking, breath held, waiting for someone to notice the drowning child.

Another wave crashed across. A leg stuck up out of the churning foam. Netta drew in a ragged breath and screamed, ran, grabbed the life guard's arm with one hand and pointed with the other. She forced herself to breathe as the child was pulled out of the waves, flopping like a large pale starfish over the shoulder of her rescuer. When the lifeguard finally found the disinterested mother, Netta watched the frightened child be admonished instead of comforted. Then the beach swirled and melt around her, and she was back standing in front of the broken piano. The heavy coin heated in her hand and faded out of existence.

'So, now you understand?' asked the old woman as she played a tinkling music-box tune on the piano that had not made a sound for decades.

'How can I have made a contract to do a thing before I, well the me now, ever existed?'

'Wishes exist outside of space and time.' The bent fingers played on gently as she explained. 'Wishes, dreams, co-incidences, serendipity, happy accidents. Throughout life, we wish and dream and desire. When those wishes and dreams reach ... let's call it critical mass, then we offer you the deal.'

'So I get to go back and help myself ... make young Netta's wishes come true?'

'Yep. If you want to.'

'What if I don't?'

'Things will be different, for Netta, for you.'

'I thought I was going to die that day.'

'Yep. Except that lifeguard happened to see your foot appear in the churning waves.' The old woman stopped playing and reached inside the skeletal piano. Her bent fingers held a bag. The coins inside jingled quietly as she handed it to Netta. 'You use each coin to pay your luck backwards.'

'What kind of a deal is that? If I don't go back the wishes don't happen?'

'Not all wishes get granted.'

'So I'll be some kind of fairy-god-mother?'

'You'll be a time traveller, Netta. Each coin is tuned-in to a wish, while you're there you'll be hypo-present. Sometimes that's problematic, but usually not.' She turned back to playing the piano.

'What happens to me here, I mean now, while I'm back in time?'

'How long do you think you were gone this time?'

Netta looked at the clock. 'No time really.'

'Times like that.'

'So how does this work?'

'Like I said, hypo-present, not fully now, but not fully then. While you're there, or then, you'll be the image in the corner of an eye, the nudge, the barely heard whisper that someone thinks of as their own good idea.'

'So it's safe?'

'Do we have a deal?'

Netta knew there were times in her life she had wished so hard and times when luck was on her side. She wondered which wishes she'd be helping to grant. The bag in her hand felt much heavier than it looked. 'We have a deal.'

The second coin deposited Netta into a patch-work of orange streetlight and tree shadow. A few metres away, the phone box looked like a photo out of the Guinness Book of Records, entitled 'fit your whole family into a phone box'. The young mum was inside with the toddler sitting on the steel phone book shelf, drawing on ripped out pages with a purple crayon. She was dropping each picture on to her much younger brother who was dozing in an umbrella pram, the young mum had somehow managed to get them all inside the phone box.

Netta saw the dark smudges on the little faces, and knew that this day must have been a vegemite day. A day when the money had run out and they'd made do with vegemite and bread, vegemite and potato, stretched thin until pay-day. Netta remembered this conversation. She remembered feeling lost and alone, standing in a little box in the custard coloured light, surrounded by darkness. She had reached out, with her last few coins, she had called her mother, she wanted comfort, reassurance that things would get better and she wasn't alone.

'Hello.'

'Hi Mum.'

'Oh. Is that you Netta?' she says like she doesn't recognise her own kid's voice.

'Yes, Mum.

'I didn't expect to hear from you.'

'Yeah, well.' She sniffles. 'I've had a really hard day.'

'You don't call very often, and it wasn't that long ago, was it?'

'I call when I can afford it. Long distance calls cost a bit of money.'

'What do you want? You only call when you want something.'

'Nothing ... I just.' She sniffles again, leaning her head back on the cool glass of the phone box wall. 'I've had a really hard day.'

'Well, what is it?'

'I wanted—'

'I knew it. You only call when you want something.'

What Netta had wanted that night was a mum. An ear, a shoulder to cry on for a little while before she walked back home through the darkness to figure out how to make dinner with the last four ingredients in her pre-payday pantry.

Money was not comfort, but she remembered when she found that cash outside the phone box that night, she had felt like the universe was on her side, even if her mother still had no idea how to offer comfort. Young Netta hung up the phone. She would stay there a while and cry quietly until the kids started fussing. Watching from the shadows, Netta wanted so badly to gather her young self into the hug she needed, but instead, she strolled out of the shadows and past the phone box dropping the two twenties as she went by. The notes fluttered to the ground, the coin heated and dissolved in her pocket and the sad evening swirled and faded around her.

Jingling music came from everywhere and nowhere. Netta reached into the bag and took the warm coin. She was all at once in a rubbish dump. This was a long time before the phone box, but as the memory rose into her mind she smiled until she laughed. This was the day she got to give herself the thing that would be the start to the greatest pleasure in her life.

The dust swirled into willy-willies. Netta blinked away the grit. When she opened her eyes, she checked to see if the cluster of blokes were busy drinking beer and solving the problems of the world, then she scuttled around searching through the piles of tangled detritus. Lifting junk and pushing aside pile after pile, urgency building as she heard burps and cans clanking into an old oil drum. Then the mumbled beginnings of good-byes. There it was, a flat tyre, a spoked wheel. Netta flipped over a rusty piece of tin – ouch!

She hauled the bike out from the tangle, jogged along behind the piles until she was at her father's ute. She whipped the tarp off the back of the ute, flung the bike in and recovered the load. Netta hunched behind a tall pile of crap, smiling and coughing up dust. She watched her father swerve his way down and out of the dump road. She knew that when he got home he'd be pretty pissed and really have no clue how the bike got there, but she'd thanked him and hugged him, and he had taken the credit for the thoughtful deed.

Netta looked down at the scratch on her hand. She wondered about getting hurt while she was 'hypo-present', but shrugged the thoughts away, remembering how young Netta's riding adventures on that rescued bike would turn into a love for cycling that would last a life-time. She smiled as the coin heated, and the dump swirled and melted away.

Over the years, the coins took Netta here and there in time in any order they pleased. She would drop a little improvised luck and love at each point in time. The bag of coins became emptier as her heart filled with satisfaction.

This time, swirling into a swaying train, Netta grabbed the hand-rail to stop herself falling, but still bumped her head. Her teen self was fast asleep using her backpack as a pillow. Netta remembered going to that football match. A night game with all her buddies, buying the beer because now she was old enough, barely. She'd had her friends to keep her awake on the train, but they got off at earlier stops. If she slept through her stop, she'd end up who knows where. Netta felt the train slowing into the station, then remembered what had woken her that night. 'This train terminates,' she boomed in a bad, something foreign, accent. 'All out, all change.'

Young Netta, startled awake, grabbed her bag and stumbled out onto the platform as the doors were about to close. 'This train terminates?' Netta laughed, rubbing the bump on her head as the train rippled away.

Another time, with the coin hot in her hand, Netta gazed around until she made sense of the bustle and noise she has appeared in. This is the train station where a twenty-something Netta had sat nervous and tired after a drawn out job interview. Her heart thumped with remembered panic as she scanned and the seats, and saw the worn yellow envelope that contained a young life worth of certificates and documents. She swooped in, clutching the envelope with sweaty hands and took it to the guard at the ticket window. She waited remembering the eternity it had seemed to take her younger self to change trains and reverse her trip that day. The train pulled in, a teary young Netta jogged up to the ticket window, gripping the counter as she spoke to guard. She clutched the precious yellow envelope, smiling with tears of relief flowing. The station swirled away.

This time, Netta arrived into darkness filled with the crying and burbling of a sleepless baby boy. Netta remembered how tired she'd been that night, sitting and holding her son while the rest of the house slept. Her younger self, slumped heavily against the lounge cushions, patting the restless boy until she was nodding off herself and then twitching awake as the baby grizzled again. It had been many hours. Moonlight cast a path of cool light across mother and child. Netta could see the trickle of exhausted tears spilling down young mother's cheeks. Netta stepped silently through the shadows until she stood over the shoulder of her exhausted younger self. She leaned in and out of the band of moonlight, pulling faces at her sleepless son until he settled and slept. Then she rearranged the pile of pillows around mum and babe so that no one could fall. 'You're a good mum,' she whispered, brushing a gentle hand across young Netta's head and the moonlit scene melted away.

Next time, the baby boy wasn't much older and, she knew, still keeping his mum up at night. So she smiled to herself when she appeared in the back corner of the little shop, watching young Netta encouraging her toddler daughter towards independence, by choosing her own sweets, while her son slept in his pram. Lollies in hand, mum and daughter turn to leave the shop. Netta leans out from the corner and rattles the toys dangling from the forgotten baby's pram. The girl turned at the noise. 'Mummy, you forgot the baby.'

Young Netta turned pink with embarrassment, rushing back for the pram. 'You're such a good big sister,' she said. One hand in her daughter's hand, the other pushing the pram through the tattered fly strip hanging in the shop doorway.

Decades later, Netta watches her young self, tossing and turning in a knot of bedsheets. She crouches in the shadow of a pile of packed boxes. She knows the boxes have been backed a long while, and waiting for the time she would be brave enough to make the big move interstate. The tossing and turning was fuel by doubt and second guessing. Young Netta wanted to know everything would be alright for her and her kids if she took them for this necessary fresh start.

Briefly, the tossing and turning had stopped. A moment or two of sleep between worry. Netta began quietly to tell the stories of all the fun and success that awaited if she would take those boxes and take the chance on that fresh start. She whispered about new friends and sunny days, a comforting new home and eventually an amazing man to share her heart with. Netta remembered that these strange, very real whispers at the edge of her waking had given her the courage she'd needed to change her life.

Netta hears the music, picks up the warm coin from the bag and arrives into darkness. She takes a breath. The air is thick with humid summer blossoms and she remembers. The strained words behind her confirm her recollection and she shuddered.

Across the road, she sees the dog wander into a circle of rusty light to pee on the lamp-post. She jogs across the road, whips of her scarf, captures the dog. With a quick reassuring pat, she tugs the dog back across the road and into the darkness to where, she knows, young Netta is wishing hard.

In the dark shadows of the bushes in the back corner of the park, the sounds of struggle and pleading fill the humid air. Netta remembers this date that was ending so horribly. She remembers how nice it had been to have all this guy's attention on that warm, romantic night. The walk in the park on the way home that had twisted into a frightening betrayal of trust. There was a slap and then the tears. The dog at Netta's side growled.

She walked towards the sounds in the darkness. The dog growled again. 'What is it, Bonzo,' she said, but remembering with a shudder that the young date-monster had grabbed young Netta tight and held his hand over heard mouth to stop her seeking help. The dog growled more deeply. Netta clenched her teeth, made a twisting smile and let the dog free of the scarf.

The growling dog bounded into the bushes, the young date-monster screamed and ran. Netta ran into the bushes towards her young self. 'Are you alright?' she asked holding the trembling girl. She led young Netta out of the bushes and they watched the dog chase the date-monster across the street and through the pool of rusty light, where the dog lost interest and returned to his lamp-post.

'I'll walk you home,' said Netta. All her trembling younger self could do was nod. At the familiar letterbox, young Netta croaked out a shaky thank you. Netta leaned hard on that letter box remembering how scared and grateful she had been that night. As her young-self slipped silently into the house, it all faded away leaving nothing but her heart thumping in her chest.

Years of remembering and forgetting and growing old had happened to Netta. All the while, one last coin remained unused, but the music never came. From time to time, Netta would find the coin and hold it, but nothing would happen. She'd laugh and wonder what she'd do if the coin did call her. How would she be able to make good on her last part of the deal to help young Netta when she could barely help herself?

The doctors and the carers didn't have to say it, pain told Netta that her life was drawing to a close. Sickness and pain had faded Netta's life into a sluggish shadow. She sat nestled, small in the over-stuffed armchair, and reached to rub the last coin, which she had decided turned into a necklace. A reminder of her secret and extraordinary life. She had made a deal with the strange old piano player and she'd had the precious chance to offer herself love and kindness, which had changed the course of her life. But lives, no matter how full of love and luck, well end.

Tinkling music roused Netta from sleep. She groaned and coughed, struggled to catch her breath, waking from a dream of being tumbled in that huge wave all those years ago.

'We had a deal.'

Netta turned her head, wiping tears from her eyes, she saw the old lady and the broken piano. Netta clutched at the last coin. 'I know we had a deal, but how can I be helpful now?'

'The coins were all for you Netta,' the old woman said as she played.

The coin warmed up between Netta's bent fingers. The room and the music faded. Everything was warm and green. She felt scratchy fabric against her cheek. Netta was laying on her side, curled up and all the pain was gone. She remembered the scratchy fabric and the cinnamon-apple smell of her grandmother. Then a warm crinkled hand landed lightly and stroked her hair.

'Granny.'

'Yes, Sweety, shh, shh. Time to sleep.' Her grandmother sang quietly. Netta hadn't thought of that lullaby for so long. Her grandmother's voice mingled with piano music. The coin cooled in Netta's hand as she sunk her head into the softness of her Granny's lap and fell asleep for a final time.

16

Ever-Rain

'Rain, rain, go away, and don't come back another day.' Ellis heard herself humming the old childhood rhyme. Her family told her the rhyme used to be different, but now children never wished for rain, they never had to. For Ellis and her generation, it had never stopped raining.

Ellis listened to the WeatherCast on the vid screen as she hunched off her dry-pack and pushed it into the storage alcove, '...9490 days without sunshine,' the report droned on, saying what it always said.

'Twenty-six years since SunTime,' she said as she entered the kitchen. 'Why don't they just say twenty-six years?'

Aunt Meg looked up from the stunted vegetables she was dicing. 'Playing with the words I guess. Maybe they think saying *days* sounds like less time than years.' She shrugged. 'However you say it, it's still raining.' She returned to the vegetables.

'Surely the Sun's rays are reaching the ground somewhere,' said Ellis as she watched.

'WorldCouncil say the Cloud was everywhere.' Aunt Meg sighed.

'So what good does it do to watch a Weather-Cast?' Ellis shut off the vid screen.

'People are hopeful, so they watch and hope.'

'What about the others? They stand dripping on the street corners, holding their smashed umbrellas, screaming, "The Sun is shining out there." And yelling all those random numbers. They're more crazy than hopeful.'

'They believe, Ellis. They want it to be different from the mess you've inherited.'

'Searching for an edge would be impossible anyhow,' said Ellis. 'Even travelling to the end of the train lines you're still under the Cloud, and planes stopped flying when they banned fossil fuels, so how would you travel on past the last train stop? No matter how hopeful or curious, or crazy you were.'

'Hey, this is a happy day. Don't concern yourself wondering if the Cloud had an edge. You've got your internship. You're on your way, Ellis. One day you'll see the sun from up on a Tower.'

'What if the cloud did have an edge? Then you could see a full moon again and we could go to the beach.' Ellis lifted the old photo book from the coffee table, flipping through scenes of a different, sunny world, a much younger aunt, with Ellis's parents smiling in the sunshine.

'I know how important it is to you.' Aunty Meg wrapped Ellis in a warm hug. 'I know you'll make a difference one day.'

'But they won't get to be on the beach again.' She brushed her fingers over her parents faces and closed the book.

'They'd be so proud of you, but I'm proud enough for us all.' Meg squeezed Ellis and pecked her cheek. 'Why don't you do some time on the bike, generate some watts, burn off some energy.'

'Do my bit for the good of the city,' Ellis chirped, sounding like the motivation messages on the vid screen.

'Yeah, yeah, all that.' Meg laughed 'I'll get started on your special dinner.' Meg returned to the tiny kitchen and lifted a limp, and roughly plucked bird above her head.

'Real chicken? That must have cost so much,' said Ellis starting to pedal.

'And you're worth every credit.' Meg blew Ellis a kiss and lay the scrawny chicken on the sink.

Very few animals could be raised now. To get real meat you needed to be cashed up and know which basement or apartment had been turned into a micro-farm. So, accept for special occasions, everyone ate protein that was produced in the amino vats, and then transformed, by creative molding and adding mystery spices, to make unconvincing facsimiles of burgers, fillets and other sad replicas of meat. Ellis's mouth watered at the idea of real chicken.

'We can't eat vat-splodge today, not when we're celebrating your success,' Meg said.

That success at intermediate college had earned Ellis her internship. Now she would study at university and work at Tower27 – Groundside Control, monitoring and cleaning to begin with, along with safety drills and EvacSuit protocols to prepare for working up on the Platforms one day.

Dinner that night was indeed a feast. Ellis savoured the crispy skin of the stunted roast chicken.

'We used to eat chicken all the time when we were young,' Aunty Meg said, licking her fingers, 'when we went to the beach.'

'I feel a story coming on,' said Ellis.

'Well, you opened the album. And we both miss them, especially on special days, when awesome nieces achieve amazing things.'

Ellis listened and licked her fingers, not wanting to waste one molecule of the chicken.

'Sometimes the Sun would heat the sand until it was scorching,' Aunt Meg began. 'We'd run down towards the waves feeling as though our feet were melting, then plunge them into the cool, fizzing water.' Meg's eyes stared off to that far away time. 'It was delightful.'

Ellis had never thought of water as delightful.

'But in autumn it was different, the Sun was cooler,' Meg continued. 'Then you could lay on the warm sand for hours, and stare up at the endless expanse of bright blue. The only clouds in the sky back then were fluffy and white like the ones people painted in children's stories books, fairytale clouds. We sometimes tried to see different shapes – animals and things in the cloud configurations.'

Ellis had only ever seen one Cloud configuration.

'In summer our skin tingled with the heat from the Sun beating down on us, like it was trying to cook us while we played.' Meg said. 'So our parents would make us wear sun-block.'

'Sun what?' asked Ellis.

'Sun-block. It was a greasy white cream. You spread it on your skin and it protected you from the Sun.'

'From getting cooked?' asked Ellis.

'Not really, well sort of.' Meg shrugged. 'The Sun's rays could do damage to your skin that could lead to cancer.'

'So tell me again why you loved the Sun so much,' Ellis said sarcastically.

'Ice-cream.' Meg smiled. 'We all loved ice-cream. We'd always get ice-cream after lunch. Then we would sit in the shade of the trees, or under a huge umbrella, racing to eat it before it melted. It would always melt before we could finish, trickling down your chin and dripping from your elbow.'

The reality for Ellis was that the only dripping and trickling at the beaches was the endless rain and the risen seas washing everything away. The beaches her aunty spoke of, only existed in old family albums. There are no Sun umbrellas any more.

Ellis came out of the kitchen, after cleaning up the feast and saw Meg was staring out the window.

'Full moon tonight?' she asked.

'Yeah,' Meg sighed. 'It's still there, even if you can't see it.'

Ellis knew Meg had fallen in love at the beach. She'd heard the story of how lovers sat on chilly rocks, tangled up in each other's arms, listening to the gentle surf, watching the full moon rise, fat and creamy-yellow over the ocean, making pearls of moon-light on the water. The lovers had sat talking together all night long, and at dawn they'd watched the sun creep up, golden and radiant, casting diamonds on the still water.

None of these memories were Ellis's. She gently touched the curled and faded photos of mythical beach holidays. Tomorrow she would start at Tower27 and one day she would go up and see the Sun with her own eyes, then she would have her own memories.

The awkward pile of rain gear tumbled from the locker and slumped on the shining lobby floor. Ellis sighed and sat down on the chair, untangled the pants from the pile and pushed her legs into them. The crinkly bulkiness made her feel heavy.

'Good morning, Ellis,' said Sid from behind his desk.

'Morning, Sid,' she said as she pushed her slippered feet into knee high rain boots. She tucked the pants in to the boots to smooth them, then zipped the seal joining them.

'Enjoying the new job?' he asked.

'It's been great so far.'

'So, when do you go up?' asked Sid, smiling.

Ellis pulled on her calf-length coat, took her dry-pack and face shield and moved to Sid's desk.

'I wish it could be now,' she said as she zipped her jacket seal and fixed the hood in place. Lowering her voice, she said, 'I watch the monitors when no one's looking. I saw the sun. It was amazing, it blazed right out of the screen.'

'It sure was amazing, Ellis, before old *dark and stormy* changed everything.' Sid pointed a finger skyward. 'If you think the Sun looks good on screen, you should feel it shining on you in person. Made your skin prickle, and it warmed you right down to your bones.' He laughed. 'Then those greedy fools made their mess and broke the weather. Now all we have is cloud.' He smiled.

'Look on the bright Ellis-girl, pardon my pun, but if the Cloud was gone, then, no one would need a SealMan to keep the indoors dry now would they, and I'd be out of a job.' Sid hit the button and the door seal started cycling open.

'I'll go up one day, Sid.' She waved and pulled the hooded visor over her head. 'Maybe soon,' she whispered to herself as she headed out to her bike to slosh her way to Tower27.

Pulling her bike out of the building's lockers, she checked its generator mode and took a deep breath and sealed her face shield. Riding the Sub-Trains was expensive, so people rode bicycles most of the time. Ellis hopped onto her bike and rolled out to join the swarm of peddling commuters weaving past each other. There was a constant flow of shallow water across the road, and with their RainGear slick and shiny, the cyclists looked like a flock of dull coloured wind-up peacocks spraying up continuous fan-tails of water behind them us the wheels churned in the puddles.

Ellis looked up at the Cloud and surveyed the permanent twilight of her city. She could see Tower27 in the distance. It rose like the stem of a giant steel beanstalk, stretching iup above the high raise housing blocks until it disappeared into the blanket of grey. The Tower was constructed of a series of segments woven together, like an enormous Chinese finger puzzle. Each interwoven section engineered to work together, sliding against each other so that it could lengthen and shorten with the change in the Cloud's level. This engineering allowed the Tower to be kept at the correct altitude so that the Platform, and the solar banks, would always be in the sunshine above the Cloud.

Up ahead, Ellis noticed the shredded umbrella, held by a man yelling to everyone passing by. He was saturated. Ellis wondered what happened to people who couldn't afford to buy RainGear. Maybe they dissolved or rotted? Who would notice anyway? Living under the Cloud makes you keep your head down, hunched against the rain. Everyone rode by ignoring the yelled stream of numbers until the man shoved his umbrella out into the flow of bikes. People swerved to avoid the umbrella, then swerved to avoid other bikes. Ellis wasn't quick enough to avoid a collision. She glanced into a back wheel that crossed her path, the bike careened into a deeper puddle, causing murky water to spray up and over Ellis in a grey wave.

As her visor cleared she saw the umbrella, heard the yelled numbers. Then Ellis, her bike, the umbrella and the crazy guy were tangled on the footpath. Ellis's heart pounded. She sat catching her breath. The number yeller pulled free of the tangle. Yelled the number series into her face-shield. 'When you want to know more, you'll find us in the Floaties.' He grabbed her and shoved something into the pocket of her jacket. Then he snatched up his umbrella and disappeared into the gloom.

Heart thumping, she picked up her bike from the road-side, checking it and her rain gear for damage. The man was gone, but she was scared. She'd never gone out the *Floaties*, where the poorest people existed, floating on pontoons in the swamp. She looked at the object. It was a piece of plastic with numbers scratched into it. She slid it back into her pocket. Did the guy yell the numbers because he was nuts? Or did he know something that made him crazy? What if the numbers were a real message somehow?

As she rode on she thought of the old Sun-Time stories. Maybe if Meg had kept the stories to herself she would find it easier to ignore the crazy number yellers and then she wouldn't find it impossible to wait to go up the tower, but the stories and the old photos created a hunger in Ellis that she could no longer ignore. She wanted to feel the Sun on her face, to see the stars piercing the black velvet of heaven, to feast on a creamy full moon. She'd wave to the man in the moon and he'd wave back, well that was what she thought when she was younger.

Working in maintenance at Tower27, Ellis was almost invisible. She could look over the shoulders as the GroundTeam received data and scheduled Tower adjustments and relayed updates to the TowerTeam up on the Platform.

One afternoon, as she did her usual waste-paper bin run in the control room, she noticed an excited knot of conversation at one of the monitors. As usual she hadn't been noticed, so she eased in closer. She glanced over the seated technician's shoulder, at the strange sight on the monitor. Green and sunshine. It looked like a scene in the photos in the family albums. Green, grass and trees. Ellis held her breath and stared at the screen for as long as she dared then melted into the background to listen.

'How long has this been true?'

'Long enough, well since I started here, anyway.'

'But that's amazing. It's wonderful, an edge to the Cloud.

'Shhh.'

'But when people find out it will change everything.'

'The only thing I've ever seen this change is the workers here, they tend to disappear if management hears talk like that.'

'What! The WorldCouncil knows?'

'Of course they do, and they're not stupid. While we believe the Cloud goes on forever, we all run around like drowned rats, *doing our bit*, for free. We help to grow food and generate power for the city. And we don't complain when things are tough, that stops the WorldCouncil having to work too hard, or spend money.'

'People are suffering under the Cloud.'

'Not as much as we'll suffer if we say anything. You never saw anything, right?' He leaned over and flicked the monitor back to a data screen.

Ellis squeezed her hands into fists and dug her nails into her palms to check this wasn't some ridiculous dream. There was an end to the Cloud, and the WorldCouncil was keeping it a secret. People who threatened to talk about it disappeared. Ellis felt hot with anger at being denied an alternative to rotting under the Cloud, and having that knowledge hidden.

She wanted to run and tell someone—everyone. She thought of the crazy, number-yelling man. She wanted to scream it out too.

'Kim, can we go for coffee this afternoon?' she asked her friend.

'Sounds nice,' said Kim as she pried Ellis fingers from where they were gripping her arm. 'Is everything okay?'

'It's just—I—I have to tell someone—' She trailed off.

'Let's finish a bit early then.' said Kim. She rubbed Ellis's shoulder and smiled. 'We can go to the CafeDome.'

They collected their bags and scanned out through security, put on their RainGear and wheeled their bikes down the soggy block. The CafeDome boasted being a *rain-positivity* business. The whole place was fully enclosed in a rain-proof dome and lit with blazing bulbs that attempted to conjure up sunshine. The place was set up as a SunTime sidewalk café, with a central kiosk surrounded by clusters of tables and chairs. It even had potted plants, fake of course, just like the coffee they sold.

Ellis and Kim ordered synth-coffee and sat towards the edge of the dome. The rain falling on the outside made glittering ribbons as it flowed to the sidewalk. You couldn't see much of the street outside but that helped complete the illusion.

'What's wrong, girl?' asked Kim after the coffee arrived.

'I found something out, I saw something today. It's amazing and horrible.' Ellis was stirring a hole in the bottom of her coffee cup, deciding if she should really say anything.

'It's okay. You can tell me.' Kim reached for Ellis's hand.

'I saw green. I saw Sun shining on the ground. It was on the monitors,' she whispered harshly.

'I see,' said Kim. 'I've heard they play that joked on newbies. I just wondered when they'd do it to us.'

'No Kim, it wasn't like that, they didn't know I was there. They were arguing about it. Maurice was threatening the other tech and warning her not to say anything. He said she would really regret it if she did.'

'But Ellis, it just can't be true. Why would they keep that kind of knowledge a secret?'

'I feel like I should do something or talk to someone.'

'You're right, Ellis. I think it'd help to talk to someone. Maybe the counsellor back at campus. Internships can be really stressful.' She squeezed Ellis's hand. 'But you'll be okay.'

'No. I mean tell someone. Get the proof so they'll believe us and tell people, maybe post it on the VidNet.'

'There's no *us* here, Ellis. This is all your idea, and you need get over it before you wreck your chances of getting onto a TowerTeam.' Kim smiled. 'Come on drink up, then we can head to campus. I'll help you tell the counsellor if you're embarrassed about being stressed out.'

Ellis froze and rethought before she went too far. She realized that Kim was not going to listen or believe, and if she got too spooked by Ellis's ideas then she would tell Maurice and that would be the end of her plan to go up-tower. She knew Kim would not help her, not knowingly anyway. Ellis held Kim's hand and took a shuddering breath, which she hoped Kim would interpret as relief rather than frustration.

'You're such a good friend,' Ellis said in a sing-song voice. 'Yeah, I am a bit stressed I guess. Hey don't tell them that they got me with that joke, I'd die of embarrassment.' She put her face in her hands to hide her poor acting and fake smile.

'Of course. What are friends for,' said Kim. 'Do you still want to see the counselor?'

'I do,' she lied. 'Will you come with me, like you said, maybe Tuesday? We've got to go campus then anyway.'

'Great idea,' said Kim, smiling kindly.

Ellis smiled back, sipping the coffee that was as fake as her words. She vowed again to do whatever she needed to do, to end the secret keeping and suffering. She conjured her plan as she sat sipping and smiling.

The TowerTeam maintained the links from the Platform. They monitored *weather* and transmitted adjustments for Platform height in relation to Cloud height to gain maximum exposure for solar panels. They relayed data and Groundside Control and together they kept the Platform operating with maximum efficiency.

Kim had forgotten all about counselors after a few days, but Ellis had continued making plans since the day she saw edge of the Cloud on the live-feed monitors. There were only ever four people in a TowerTeam on the platform, so there would be more chance to access the data up there than down at Groundside.

Regardless of all her planning, she was chilled by one thought, what would the penalty be if she was caught? She couldn't think about that. Before she'd seen the monitor, she had fantasied about sneaking up to feel the Sun on her face, and grabbing a few selfies of her with the moon, and later a sunrise in the background. But now, she had to get the data she needed to show all the sodden people under the Cloud what the WorldCouncil had done. She wanted to show them there was an alternative, a place for them were the Sun warmed the ground and the world was still green, out there somewhere.

Ellis continued making plans. She studied Tower schematics, learned how the security routines worked, and took advantage of the technician's carelessness to collect passwords and entry codes. Finally, she had everything she thought she needed, and knowing access to the truth was there at the top of the Tower made it impossible to wait. Tonight there'd be a full moon, so she would at least achieve her goal of seeing the moon and feeling the sun on her face in the morning, if she lasted that long undetected. And if she could access to the data feed, she would use that information to change everything for everyone under the Cloud. She couldn't wait any longer.

The TowerTeam was dressed in their Evac-Suits as they walked to the elevators. Ellis and Kim watched them. The four team members weighed in with their packs as they waited for the elevator doors time-lock to release. Minimum personnel were allowed on the Platform because of the weight limits.

'That will be us one day, Kim,' said Ellis. She nudged her friend, and as she did she slipped her ID tag into her pocket. Kim smiled and looked down at her watch.

'We're all finished for today,' she said. 'Let's go.'

'Oops, I left my vid book in the locker room,' stammered Ellis.

'Okay, see you in three,' said Kim, as she walked towards the front door. When she moved through the security point, the computer registered two interns leaving Tower27. They were not scheduled again for three days, and aunt Meg thought Ellis was staying at Kim's for a couple of nights to study.

GroundSide would do a census sweep once every twenty-four hours to detect any uninvited visitors by measuring for extra mass. This happened at *sunrise* every day, so Ellis would have one impossible day to find all the information she needed to convince people there was an edge to the Cloud. And, of course, to get her photographs before the sirens would signal her presence.

Ellis waited inside the service room until she was sure no one would walk by, she nervously approached the security door, entered the access code from her SwingDrive into the lock for the emergency stairs and slipped in unseen. Easing the door closed silently behind her, she let out the breath she'd been holding. Above her, the tower stretched up until she could only see a narrowing blur.

The metal helix of the stairs twisted around the elevator shaft lengthening and shortening as the tower changed its height. The gap between the steps leading up was small, that meant the platform was thankfully lower in the sky today. The CloudTop must be down, under 2000 metres. She released her grip on the door, and wiped her sweety, shaking hands on her pants. Hoisting the ShiftPack onto her back, and clutching the bundled up EvacSuit, she put a hesitant foot on the first step.

There were no sensors on the stairs because their constant adjusted to CloudHeight would keep setting off false alarms. All Ellis needed to watch out for was people leaving the elevator at an escape point if there was an emergency, the new team was long gone but the returning team would head down after a two hour debrief. If the downward TowerTeam evacuated into the tower stairs it would be all over.

The endless left turn of the stairs threatened to overwhelm Ellis with dizziness. She gripped the railing and hoped it would ease soon, distracting herself by going over her plan. She would easily get to the platform well before sunrise, then she'd have to wait until the dawn census sweep before she left the tower stairs. After that she'd need to avoid visual detection, but she knew the TowerTeam didn't go out on the ledge too much, the Sun was no big deal to them now, and she knew from observing the monitors that the TowerTeam didn't get down-time except for sleep and meals.

The twisting stalk of the metal stairs finally ended. Ellis was exhausted. She took an AminoCake from her ShiftPack and ate, washing the crusty meal down with some warm bottled water. Then, once she had cooled down, she shook out the EvacSuit and squirmed her way into it, fastened it closed, she checked the glide vents were intact.

With hours still remaining until dawn and the census sweep, all she could do was wait. So, just inside the hatch leading out to the Platform, Ellis curled her arms and legs through the curving stair-railings to stop herself from falling *if* she did manage to sleep. She let her eyes close and images of the twisting stairs made her head swim until she thought she would throw up her meagre meal. To ease her stomach, she tried to imagine the beach and the sunshine in the family photos. Finally, she drifted off, and slept fitfully, fearful she'd sleep too long and waste even a second of the precious day to come.

At last—sunrise plus one minute. There would not be another census sweep for nearly twenty-four hours. Ellis pushed up the hatch that opened onto the ledge surrounding the Platform's dome. An explosion of sparkling yellow-white light blasted her face. She clambered onto the narrow, circular ledge. Her eyes watered from the brightness, then real tears. Tears of amazement and awe.

Ellis squinted and stared at the top edge of the golden disc as it rose and swelled up over a field of crimson and tangerine cloud. She never thought she'd ever look at the Cloud and think it was beautiful, not from underneath anyhow.

The field of cloud rippled with ever-changing colour as the Sun rose higher, purples faded to crimson and orange to yellow. Engaging Vid on her SwingDrive, Ellis turned around slowly, capturing the melting colours, wanting to collect every image she could see for a new family album.

As she turned, she felt the Sun touch her, each arm, leg, shoulder was bathed with an amazing warmth. The heat penetrated deep into her tried muscles. She understood now why Meg retold SunTime stories, and why she needed to keep this memory alive. If the monitor information was true, then Meg would be able to feel the Sun again and so could everyone else.

The cloud-sea of candy colours had faded leaving endless, blinding white, Ellis focused on her plan to get the data she needed. She would access the Platform relays and search for anything that would give her hard evidence that the Cloud had an edge. But, that could wait a little longer, the Sun had her in its spell.

Ellis sat, letting the warmth soak into her. She breathed deeply as if she could breathe in this amazing radiance and collect it to have with her until her life could be free of the Cloud. She watched mesmerized for hours as the blazing orb slowly arced across the sky. Ellis could hear Aunt Meg's beach stories in her mind, and she imagined taking the train, or riding, or walking all the way to that sunny green place she had spied on the monitors.

Sharp metallic footsteps bought Ellis back from her imaginings. She scrambled wildly into the shadows of a storage alcove next to the stairway hatch. Her head collided with a low partition wall. Pain flared and her ears rang. Hidden, holding her breath she tried not to cry. Wild blotches of colour danced behind her eyes-lids until the pain faded.

The technicians walked past, too busy talking to notice her. She was the last thing they would ever have expected to see up here. Ellis felt a warm trickle of blood running down from her temple. 'Stupid,' she whispered to herself. She sat, feeling dizzy in the shadows, too scared to move.

The Sun had almost completed its arc across the sky when Ellis finally crept out of hiding. The light had faded, creating another glorious soup of radiant colours in the west. She turned and saw the Moon rising, creamy and swollen. It looked larger than the Sun had this morning but she knew that was not the case. She must find out how that illusion happens later, if she gets the chance. Her plans for getting off the tower were very theoretical. Ugly what-ifs about her plan to get back down crowded in on her.

She shook the thoughts clear from her mind and turned to the Moon's crater-face that seemed to be smiling down at her. She'd dreamt of seeing the *man in the moon* when she was young. She waved at *him*, smiling to herself, and that helped to push the last anxiety from her mind.

Beyond the Moon were countless stars piercing the velvety blue-black. She turned slowly, staring, her breath caught in her throat. Lifting her SwingDrive, she captured images of the immense sea of stars. Stretching out her arm, she made sure she caught her own face next to the smiling Moon to show she had really been here.

Finally, she shut off her SwingDrive and cautiously moved inside the dome. There were no adjustments needed for the solar-panels at night, so this section was empty. At a console, she located the satellite mapping function, and began searching.

It was difficult to work the consoles with only moon-light to illuminate the controls. Ellis fumbled and double-checked each command. For hours, image after endless image, flicked across the data screens. She carefully scanned them all, and rejected them all in turn. She felt time running out. She felt overwhelmed, foolish not to have considered the countless data-feeds stretching out across the planet. The Moon had climbed high in the blackness behind her. 'I've risked too much to fail.' She stifled an exhausted sob.

Her legs folded beneath her as she realised she was finally looking at – green! Cloud shadow, but beyond it, sunlight shining on green. 'Yes!' She had found the edge. It wasn't just some Ground-side trick. Ellis could hear her heart pounding in her ears. She quickly geo-labeled the images and stored them on her SwingDrive, then carefully shut down the console, ensuring she removed any traced of her hacked search.

Staggering back out onto the platform ledge, her mind was swimming with realization, and joyous possibility. Sun—warming the ground. Sun! Ellis stared out at the stars again and then sat herself in a pool of moonlight and reviewed the data on her SwingDrive. The Cloud had an edge. Why keep it a secret? The TowerTeams knew. Why don't they tell? Why wouldn't the WorldCouncil announce the Cloud had an edge? What would happen to the city if people did find out?

Ellis understood people power, citizens produced the food and generated the power. They kept the city alive. If lots of people rode away past the edge of the Cloud to see the Sun, the city would stop?

'People have a right to know,' she whispered. 'They should be able to feel the Sun on their skin and watch the Moon rise, to be free from the mould and the damp. I will tell them – if I—' She shuddered, and thought nervously about emergency evacuation procedures, to be used if TowerTeam needed to get off the Platform quickly for some reason. She wondered if she could really do it. There was no alternative, she couldn't go back down through the tower, security had already logged her out more than a day ago—there was no other way.

Ellis found a sheltered spot on the ledge, leaned her head against the cool metal of the dome. She ran her hands along the folded glide-panels on her EvacSuit and stared up at the Moon, as she tried to slow her breathing.

The bright light glowing through her closed eye lids woke Ellis. She had dreamed of Icarus. The sunlight washed over her. As she stretched, the alarm sounded. Her extra weight had triggered the CensusSweep alert. It would only be minutes until the TowerTeam scanned the Platform and found her. Her heart pounded.

'Everything I know is all on my SwingDrive,' she said. 'Aunt Meg is the only one with access to it, if I—.'

Ellis rushed to un-zip the opening in her Evac-Suit and shoved the precious SwingDrive into the pocket at the pocket of her jeans. Refastened the suit, pulled the goggles on to her eyes and tightened the strap. She pulled the sheer, polymer glide-panels from their storage pockets on the undersides of the suit's arms. Rushing to attach the panels to anchor points that ran down the sides of her body to her ankles to form flimsy wings. She stared into the Sun, soaking up the diamonds of light until her eyes stung and flooded with tears.

'One way or another,' she said, 'I will let everyone know that the Cloud does not go on forever.'

Ellis heard shouting behind her. She stood tall, no hunching any more. Everyone hunched under the Cloud, but soon that would change. She tilted slowly and dived into the rays of the rising Sun. spreading the glide-wings of her EvacSuit, she floated there for the briefest moment. The voices behind her faded and as she swooped away from the platform. Now she had the sky to herself, she thought of Icarus again. She spun and tumbled as sunshine washed over her like sparkling caramel. Then she tucked and dived back under the Cloud.

The cloud was a thick gray tangle, wet and cloying against Ellis's face. She tumbled wildly and her breath jagged as she tried to take control of the glide wings. Her arms finally won the fight and she managed to spread the wings out fully. This slowed her decent, but she was still blinded by the grey floss that surrounded her. All she could do was remember her glide training and hold her posture, maintain the open wings, how long would she fall through the cloud? And then what would she do? Loaded onto her SwingDrive were coordinates that showed the edge of the cloud that was closest to the city. It was a long way. Ellis's arms ached and burned, the wings buffeted and billowed as she glided downwards in the greyness. Drops of water joined into trickles that formed an icy web across her face. She shivered and her teeth chattered violently.

There were lights now, the lights of the sodden city below were slowly brightening as the cloud thinned. These moments of damp uncertainty, as

Ellis glided through the clouds, had given her time to decide. She wanted Meg to have this amazing knowledge, but how could she return home now? As soon as they realised she was the one who breached the tower, they would come for her. Would she disappear like all the crazies who had called numbers in the crowded streets?

Ellis banked, circling anti-clockwise as the glide drill had trained her to do. She watched the sodden city below. The wet streets shone like the bars of an enormous cage. She had completed a full circle of the tower now and could see the glow of the recovery area, pale green fluoresce on the Groundside Control rooftop as she continued her baking spiral.

Beyond the crisscross of lit streets was the irregular darkness of the Floaties. Each tiny dot of light weaving through the inky wetness was a person, with nothing to do but rot and nothing to hope for except the edge of the cloud.

Ellis saw the tracking light blinking in the centre of her chest. She would need to remove it, then the recovery team would chase the blinking beacon and be ready to scrape what was left of her up from the street so that her broken body wouldn't cause the commuters to crash. She allowed her arm to pull inward and wrenched the beacon from the EvacSuit, immediately she started spinning out of control.

She used the force of the spin and flung the beacon away, then she strained with the last effort she could gather and spread her arms out again. The glide wings flapped erratically. She gritted her teeth and waited. The wings billowed out and stabilized. Ellis rolled her shoulder over, using her body weight to turn and she banked away from the retrieval site, the tower and the city, gliding towards the Floaties.

17

The Lamp

Relishing the relief that comes with the cool evening breeze, Sandy sat at her desk, her elbows wading through the flotsam of stationery and papery drifts of partially realised ideas. A tide of caramel light flowed across the desk to fill the corners of the small study, spilling over miss-matched crags of furniture and lapping up against a cliff of shelved books.

Concentration broken, she stared at the lamp. Tears blurred her vision. Images of now, drifted and were replaced with misty reminders of then. Why didn't she see the warning signs? Almost a year ago, at his father's funeral. She'd heard his comments, to her, and whichever well-wishers offered hugs and platitudes.

'I'll be buried not cremated — None of this religious shit.'

'Make sure no one's sober — I want my last party to be my best.' He had always enjoyed talking on topics that stirred sensibilities.

Wakes often motivated people to plan hypothetical funerals, and Sandy heard others joining in, mumbling plans for their own final farewells into their beers. Vowing to avoid religious stereotypes and discussing photos and music to carefully curate their loved-ones' heartache. She brushed all these aside along with her husband's funerary ramblings.

They say that eight out of ten people give warning signs. But what did those warning-signs look like? He was often doing things that were odd. Like his new friendship with Jim, a taxidermist. When she'd asked him why, he said, 'Just because I can.' Then he added, 'Jim's showing me some of his trade secrets. You know, all the ins and outs.' He'd laughed. 'You never know when the dog might go.'

He'd always said and done things to get reactions, but now, Sandy saw, with the with laser-focus of hindsight, which things had been warning signs. There was the phone-calls that he wouldn't talk about. And, on that last day, he was unusually cheerful.

It was school holidays, and he'd arranged for the kids to spend a few days with Nanna. With kisses all round they bundled kids and bags into his mother's car. Smiles and waves as the car shrank into the distance. Then he turned his goofy smile-waving on her. 'You'll be late for work.' He opened her car door. She watched in the rear-vision mirror as his disconcerting smile-wave faded behind her.

After work, she was greeted by the dog sitting, tail thumping, on the veranda. The house was quiet and empty. On the table was a note written with a shaky hand.

I LOVE YOU

I'M SORRY I'M SICK

I DON'T WANT YOU TO SEE ME

*ROTTING AWAY LIKE DAD DID.
I CAN'T DO THAT TO YOU SO I'M GOING
I'LL WRITE I LOVE YOU xx*

What! How sick is he? Where's he gone? Mongrel! What happened to better or worse? He'd better be sick or I'll kill him when I find him.

I'm sick. What did that mean? She'd deserved to know, to be able to hold his hand through this, whatever it is. Mongrel!

Yelling at the doctor hadn't helped, except she'd felt better to yell at someone for a moment. 'He must have gone to another GP,' the doctor had said. 'He's only ever asked me for help with his insomnia. He said he'd been driving you crazy prowling the house at night.'

'He never prowled the house at night.' She'd wept realizing he'd used her in his lie. 'So you prescribed sleeping pills?'

'A mild dose.'

'I never saw him take any pills.' She showed the doctor the note. 'He says he's sick ... would these *mild* pills be enough to ... be harmful?'

The doctor had nodded slowly. 'If I had known—'

'It seems he didn't want anyone to know.'

Sandy sat in the caramel pool of light, replaying, re-interpreting the past year with the pointless clarity of hind-sight. She paused on one scene following his visit to acquire his fifteenth tattoo. 'Another frigging dragon,' she'd said when he'd lifted the gauze.

'It's not the images that are important it's the experience, the sensation – the sting – the burn' he'd said.

'Yeah, yeah, but why always the dragons?' She'd touched the interlocking hearts tattooed on his chest. 'You've got me and the kids here surrounded by all those dragons ready to attack us.' The first tattoo was a love token, but tattooing changed into an obsession. 'Couldn't you collect something else? The maggots will slay those dragons when you're in the ground.' They'd both laughed at that.

Four days after he'd disappeared, a large envelope arrived in the mail. Local postmark—no clue there. It contained smaller envelopes marked for the daughter, the son, his mother, and herself. She ripped hers open.

I'M SORRY — I LOVE YOU

No explanations, just apologies and then instructions.

GIVE MUM THE LETTER—AFTERWARDS
KEEP THE KIDS LETTERS UNTIL THEY'RE
OLDER. I KNOW YOU, YOU'LL KNOW THE
RIGHT TIME TO PASS THEM ON
AT SOME SPECIAL TIME.

She'd touched the words—*I know you.* Brittle laughter mixed with her tears. He knew her and she didn't know him at all.

IT'S BECAUSE I'VE SHARED MY LIFE
WITH YOU THAT I FEEL I'VE DONE
ENOUGH. I DON'T WANT TO BE AN
UN-PERSON, FADING OUT IN
SOME HOSPITAL BED.
DOING IT THIS WAY — MY WAY,
SO YOU'LL REMEMBER ME AS I WAS
FOREVER. I'M DOING IT THIS BECAUSE
I LOVE YOU xx

She always thought they'd grow old together. Old and wrinkly and still in love. Mongrel! Didn't he see he was cheating her. She loved him, illness couldn't take that away, but he'd taken it away. This choice was not for her. It was for him.

Late in the evening of the seventh day. The dog signaled the arrival of two blue uniforms. The police confirmed her identity and spouted a few uncomfortable clichés, then to the crux. 'I'm afraid we have some unfortunate news, madam.'

Madam. She pictures herself wearing something low-cut, black, cleavage-y. Her sense of humour always had bad timing.

'There's been a fire at the motel where your husband's been staying,' the first uniform said sternly. 'I'm afraid he has not survived. Asphyxiation.'

'Smoke inhalation. I'm so sorry,' said the other, kinder blue uniform.

'Where? When?'

'Up the coast. Last night.'

'A fire.' Sandy's head spun. What happened to the pills?

'It appears he was smoking in bed.' The first uniform answered her unspoken question. 'It's speculated he'd fallen asleep and—'

'Smoking is bad for your health.' She winced at this poorly timed humour.

The large, tree shaped officer smiled then coughed and stood taller. 'The autopsy has found a lethal quantity of sleeping pills in his system.' He coughed again. 'And some strange wounds on the edges of the burn-damaged skin.'

'Can you tell us anything about those wounds?' asked the kinder blue uniform.

Sandy did not know anything about those wounds that night. But now she knew. It wasn't two wounds. It was fifteen in fact. Skin neatly and carefully flayed from flesh, to become a memorial. And to stop the maggots slaying the dragons.

One day, sometime in the grief storm that followed the funeral, a package had arrived. A desk lamp. The lamp's shade was a golden, velum patchwork of dragons, surrounding, guarding three names in three hearts clustered on a field of painted burgundy roses.

Sandy, touched the delicate parchment of the lamp. The skin is warm, and she remembers the real warmth of his skin and the dragons blur in the mist of her tears.

18

The Sound Watcher

Osh roused from her daydream, knowing something was wrong. It had been a long watch-shift and she had stayed up late last night studying in preparation for her testing. She'd let her mind wonder and her eyes drop, just for a moment, but how long had that moment of distraction lasted.

All around the watch station, everything was silent. The wind-chimes had stopped. Osh looked up. The flags were limp, appearing frozen in the absence of moving air. The discorporate were nearby, too close. Osh jumped up and pulled on the ropes for the alarm bells. All around inside the walled citadel she saw people checking and securing their ear-buds.

'I was distracted,' Osh confessed to Sani the chief sound-weaver. 'I was thinking of my testing and allowed myself to daydream and let my eyes drop.'

'Be kinder to yourself, Osh,' said Sani. 'We are just flesh and blood Callans. No sound-watcher could watch the flags all the time, that's why we have the chimes as a vital standby.'

'But I'm a sound-watcher. I should be more focused.'

'You are yet to finish your testing, and I'm impressed with how focused you are on preparing.' Sani's face showed something unspoken.

'What is it?' Osh asked. 'Did the un-bodied take someone?'

'Not inside the walls.' Sani took Osh's firmly. 'Vaan hasn't returned from her hunting shift.'

Osh felt hot, dizzy. 'You must go. Save her. Before the un-bodied fully incorporates in her.'

'You will come with us,' Sani said. 'This will be your testing.'

'But, we don't test outside.'

'The test is to be a challenge to your senses and sensibilities. Is saving Vaan challenge enough for you?'

Osh could only swallow and nod her head, her heart pounding.

'Be at the gate in five minutes.'

Osh raced for her pack and met Sani and the reclamation team at the gate. They secured their ear-buds, took up their singing bowls and mallets, and walked out from the chime protected citadel, beyond the safety of the shield wall, to search for Vaan. Osh's job – her test - was to watch for the wisp, and in doing so, hold witness to the extraction. She fidgeted with her pack straps then checked and re-checked her ear buds as she followed the sound weavers into the forest.

It had been generations, since the planet was scorched by solar flares that caused the disincorporation of half its population. Through the decades, the people of Calla had learned to defend against the haunting of the un-bodied.

The presence of discorporate souls caused an absolute absence. The un-bodied stilled the air as they passed through it. An absolute quiet was the only warning of their presence. Callans had barricaded themselves behind sound walls, vigilantly watching – listening for threats of infestation – they had become skilled and cleansing the un-bodied from any Callan that was taken as a host.

There was no bird-song, no breeze. Birds fled the still air, trees appeared frozen. In the complete stillness of the forest, the search party easily heard the tree branches thrashing up ahead.

Osh saw the earbud laying in the path as they approached the tree. Then she saw Vaan dangling, kicking, spinning where she had tied herself to the branch as soon as she had realised the earbud had fallen out.

The years of training drills had worked. Vaan had secured her rope on a high branch and then tied it firmly around herself, using the well-practised skills to tie the knots behind her back. Fortunately, the un-bodied are clumsy for a long while after they buzzed into an unprotected Callan, making then very bad at untying knots.

The sound weavers circled Vaan and the tree, striking their bowls with mallets in time with their footfalls. As they sensed the perfect intersection for the sound waves, they stopped and turned to face Vaan. Each sound weaver flicked a well-practised thumb and started their bowl to turn on its spindle. The felted mallets slid against the gleaming sound bowls, emitting resonant tones. The sound flooded the clearing around the tree creating a pressure pulsing at Osh's chest. Vibration wove deep into every cell until they were unified inside the bubble of sound. At the centre of that bubble, Vaan twisted and quaked at the end of her rope.

The bowls spun faster, the vibration took control of Osh's heartbeat. Now was the time to watch for the wisp. Vaan thrashed less, then not at all. Her suspended body became a pendulum, swinging, nudged by the waves of sound.

Vaan turned on the rope and Osh saw the first glow leaking from her unprotected ear. Green, translucent, bulging as the sound pushed it out. Then it burst up. An angry tangle of energy, spinning, convulsing in the air. Osh gripped Vaan's fallen earbud and watched. The angry energy knot of the un-bodied thinned and stiffened, and finally lifted up and out of the sound bubble before it could be shattered by the vibration.

Vaan open her eyes and Osh ran towards her. The earbud was replaced and the knots untied. Osh eased Vaan to the ground and sat in a tangled embrace while the sound weavers continued to bathe them both until they declared Vaan's frequency was rebalanced.

'Congratulations, Watcher Osh.' Sani's voice interrupted their embrace. 'The sound bath and your test were successful.'

Osh had held witness to her first and most important extraction. She could not have brought herself to return to their home inside the citadel without Vaan. She would rather have removed her own ear-buds and joined her in the oblivion of possession than live without her.

19

Pigeon Day

Tuesday was always pigeon day for Mavis and Beryl. If it rained it was too hard to handle the umbrellas and the knitting needles, and beside the pigeons wouldn't be there, but this Tuesday was fine and fair.

'Do you have the breadcrumbs?' asked Mavis as they strolled towards the park.

'I crumbled our last slice,' said Beryl.

'The loaf's gone already?'

Beryl nodded.

'Are there any pennies left in the tin for another.'

'No more pennies until pension day,' said Beryl.

Life was austere for the old spinster sisters, but they managed well enough, mostly.

'Well, I'm still lucky to have a wonderful sister,' Mavis smiled and squeezed Beryl's hand.

'And we have pigeon day.' Beryl smiled back and rattled the bag of bread crumbs.

The morning was warm. The sisters settled their bony bottoms on their usual seat, poured a little tea from their thermos into two scratched tin mugs and sipped, blinking into the morning sunshine.

Before long the pigeons had spread the word and fat grey bundles of feathers hovered then landed, cooing in clusters around the sisters' feet. Mavis and Beryl smiled at each other. Pigeon day always made them smile.

They slurped the last of their tea and took out their knitting. Beryl opened the crumpled paper bag and sprinkled a few crumbs at her feet.

The pigeons cooed and shuffled and peck-peck-pecked. More fat pigeons gathered, jostling each other to get to the crumbs. Mavis sprinkled another handful of crumbs on the cobbles in between her and Beryl. The fat pigeons muscled in for the best crumbs.

'Look at those fat fellas,' chuckled Beryl.

'They're almost too fat to fly,' chuckled Mavis.

Before you could say knit-one pearl-one, the knitting needles had click-clacked and clack-clicked, and four fat pigeons ceased their cooing.

'I love pigeon day,' said Mavis, sliding one fat bird then the another off her knitting needles and into her knitting bag. She took her floral hanky and wiped the blood from the needles and handed it to Beryl, who had just de-skewered her catch and was ready to wipe her needles.

'Now our cupboards won't be bare, sister dear.'

'If it wasn't for pigeon day we'd have none,' said Mavis Hubbard.

20

We all know how this ends

I t all started at sunset. The wisps of cloud were turning pink-purple, twirls of orange at the bottoms. The evening was steamy, but the law stated that only medical and emergency facilities could use air conditioning after four pm, so we all sat outside in the slightly cooler, muggy evening air, watching the sunset and chatting. The power fizzled out, everyone shrugged it off, that happen on super-hot days. We didn't notice the clouds at first then we heard the gasps all around the skinny strip of park.

As the sun dropped from view behind the line of buildings across the river, the clouds seemed to come to life. The pinks flared, the oranges swelled and brewed, flowing up and out like lava. The purples became luminous and bubbled across the sky. The clouds heaved, boiled, spread and darkened. The pinks darkened to blood red, orange fading into slimy brown. The glowing purple stopped flaring luminous lavenders and was black. The reds and browns were black. The sky hung heavy, a starless, moonless black. We all shared the same held breath, then the clouds glowed again.

Pin-points of light ignited in the clouds above. Flicking sparks of white grew to golden bubbles. They dropped like a slow-motion fiery rain. There was shouting and screaming. People grabbed arms full of loved ones and possessions and ran for shelter. Some ran inside, some huddled under awnings and gazebos. We all watched as the fiery bubbles drifted down through the humid air.

The glowing orbs took a long time to reach the ground. They drifted unnaturally, as if by design. The hidden spectators mumbled words we never believed we say – spaceship – aliens – invasion. Our world had become a movie set. A voice in the dark said, 'We all know how this ends.' There were nervous laughs and quiet weeping from the surreal movie cast.

'It's everywhere,' said a voice from a face illuminated by a phone. Little squares glowed in the darkness as people saw the news for themselves. Everywhere. The bubbles landed and settled, then they faded and nothing happened. We watched and wondered, then went home to a troubled sleep, filled with strange noises in the dark.

Sunrise lit a different world. All around, spread almost equally apart across every unpaved space, the trees had sprouted. Squat trees, brown like wrinkled trolls with stumpy arms stretched out into the steamy morning air. With our breaths held again, we could hear the noises that had disturbed us in the night. It was the trees. A squeaking sigh, coming from them as they grew.

The next noise was the sirens, then the tramping of feet. The defenders and the thinkers and the fixers, surrounded trees here and there. Poking, pushing. Digging at roots, snipping at stumpy leaves. The trees would have none of it, but they didn't squirt blinding poison or reach to strangle their inquisitors. They just stood, strong and un-cut-able. Shovels, secateurs, scalpels, all failed to affect the stumpy trees. They sat in the morning sun growing so fast we could see and hear it. The authorities declared a wait-and-see lockdown for non-essential personnel. So, we waited and saw. By sunset, the trees were two humans tall and their troll bellies measured in metres around.

The scientists spouted inconclusive rhetoric, except for the few who monitored the air quality. They stated the drop in CO_2 was notable, but speculative. Of course, trees take in carbon, why wouldn't these fast-growing trolls be gobbling carbon as they grew fat. We stayed home and watched the trees grow, smiling as we listened to the scientists reporting the CO_2 was still dropping.

After too many days of nothing happening except the trees growing fatter, we came out into our world where everything and nothing had happened. It was business as usual except for needing to walk around the trees and getting used to not having sports fields to play on, or looking at the fractured play equipment in parks, pushed aside by the still growing trees. Hiking trails were blocked, bicycle paths had become humped and buckled adventure zones. CO_2 dropped to levels not seen since last century.

The environmentalists arranged gratitude festivals, dancing, drumming chanting for the strange trees that came down to save us from ourselves. Atmospheric carbon would no longer be our extinction event.

The festival season ended with an early and bitter autumn. We all reached deep into our closets for jumpers and jackets we had not needed to wear for years.

Scientists reported CO_2 levels hadn't been this low since the twelfth century. There was Malthusian speculation of a troll-tree induced ice-age, caused a jumper buying, prepper panic.

Long life milk and toilet paper became rare as diamonds. Home insulation was priced as though it was spun from gold.

Now the power failed because of the demand for heating which we needed after living in the super-warm for so long. Environmentalists strategized around domed gardens and frost management. The troll-trees had stopped growing up, but all through that surprising, actual winter, they swelled. Their bark stretched, smoothed, darkened. One night the trees started sighing again. It was too cold to go out and watch to see why.

In that last week of our first real winter in almost a century, the trees gasped and collapsed. Where they had stood defying all human abuse, there were now spongy, soft, brown piles. Scientists analysed the piles and reported they had nothing to report. The remains were essentially compost. No structure to examine, no roots, branches or leaves to dissect and gather knowledge from. They remained as much a mystery dead as they had been alive. The only solid trend was the CO_2 levels had stopped dropping. Of course, the troll-trees had stopped taking in carbon. The environmentalists came with buckets and wheelbarrows and trucks, and took the free troll compost into our communities. Sharing out the spent flesh of the lifesaving trees to feed our farms, and replant our play parks and sports fields. There was heart felt gratitude for the warmth that came with the sunshine of a real spring after the coldest winter for over a century. We all played our parts planting and repairing. We were very glad that, as it turned out, we were totally wrong about knowing how this would end.

'You're welcome,' was the only message sent from the skies. No explanation. But it was obvious, someone from somewhere out there, gave more of a crap about our planet and our future than we did. They used their time and resources to stop us making ourselves extinct. Now we are very motivated to show them they didn't waste their time.

<u>Acknowledgments</u>

I've found great friendship and support from the wacky crew of geniuses at the Rainforest Writing Retreat. Thank you especially to Raelene, Chris, Charmaine and Pamela.

Thanks also to my brood of Bribie writers: Lexia, Pete, Bev, Larysa and Graeme. It's wonderful to have a welcoming writerly space to share story ideas.

About the Author

Martii lives north of Brisbane, Australia, in a tin shack by the sea, catching seagulls to bake delicious pies and writing offbeat stories. She likes going on long bicycle rides with her cat, who always wears aviator goggles to stop her whiskers blowing up into her eyes as they speed down to the beach in search of mermaid eggs.

Martii's other Titles

<u>Adult anthologies</u>

'*Mile High*' appeared in Tales of Murder and Mystery, '*Two Glasses*' appeared in Short Stories of Ghosts and Graves, '*The Clockwork Prince*' appeared in Short Stories of Forest and Fantasy, and '*Perfect Man*' appeared in Charms of Love in the RWR short-story series.

'We all know how this ends' appeared in Invasion of the Saucer-Men from Mars
from Specul8 Publishing.

<u>Stories for Awesome Kids</u>

Weird Weirder Weirdest: a collection of quirky tales

Creepy Creepier Creepiest: another collection of quirky tales

Strange Stranger Strangest: the another-est collection of quirky tales

The Adventures of Isabelle Necessary

Download free kid's activities and teaching resources by following links at
https://www.linkedin.com/in/martii-maclean-16197674/

<u>Young Adult Novels</u>

If I Die Before I Wake and Tales of Blood and Fate - a duology in one volume

We of the Between

Unreal Time